eleven

eleven

patricia reilly giff

SCHOLASTIC INC.
New York Toronto London Auckland
Sydney Mexico City New Delhi Hong Kong

ISBN-13: 978-0-545-20922-9
ISBN-10: 0-545-20922-6

Copyright © 2008 by Patricia Reilly Giff.
All rights reserved. Published by Scholastic Inc., 557 Broadway, New York, NY 10012,
by arrangement with Wendy Lamb Books, an imprint of Random House Children's Books,
a division of Random House, Inc. SCHOLASTIC and associated logos are trademarks
and/or registered trademarks of Scholastic Inc.

12 11 10 9 8 7 6 5 4 3 2 1   9 10 11 12 13 14/0

Printed in the U.S.A.   40

First Scholastic printing, October 2009

To Conor Gift

eleven on February 18, 2008
with love

Eleven could be anything.

It was only two lines, after all.
It could be a month, a day, minutes.
Maybe two trees in a bare winter field.
A kid scribbling.
A house number.
It was Sam's birthday, April Eleven.
That was a good thing, a great thing,
so why was he afraid of eleven?

1
The Pipe

Never mind being afraid of eleven right now. Tomorrow was his birthday. And where had they hidden his presents? Sam hadn't found a single one yet. He'd checked every drawer, every cabinet, under the beds, and even outside in the shed.

Only one place was left to search.

Could he do it?

He was skinny but tough. Of course he could.

He didn't bother with socks, just sneakers, and pulled on his jacket over his pajamas. He lifted his bedroom window that was two stories up, squinted out at the dark world, and felt for the pipe against the wall.

It was a crazy way to get to the attic, but the only way tonight. The attic pull-down door was in his grandfather's room next to his, and Mack was sound asleep by now.

Sam grinned; he pictured himself hopping around on Mack's bed, yanking down the overhead door, which would graze Mack's nose while Sam boosted himself up to the attic.

"What? What?" Mack would mutter in his sleep.

A riot. Too bad it had to be the pipe.

Sam swung himself out the window and gripped the pipe with his hands and knees. It was colder than he expected, icy. Imagine if Mack awoke in the morning to see him plastered to the side of the house, frozen solid.

He inched his way up to the attic window. Below, just beyond the shed, was the river, a narrow band of water; it slipped over the rocks, then swirled away so the rocks reappeared like turtle backs, shiny, ridged, and black.

It made him dizzy to look down. He closed his eyes. People who drove along the road in front hardly realized that a finger of the Mohawk River bubbled along behind his building. All they saw were the windows of the three stores: Mack's Woodworking Shop; Onji's Deli; Kerala House, Anima's Indian restaurant; and their apartments above.

Sam leaned his head against his raised arms and felt the stone wall with the tips of his sneakers.

Maybe he should scramble back inside.

No, he was tough.

Slowly he turned his head; the pipe vibrated. Not a light on in any of the three apartment windows. They slept like hibernating bears.

He boosted himself up a couple of feet. Night Cat was

somewhere below, meowing up at him, Night Cat, ancient, crabby, waiting to be let in downstairs. "Wait a minute, will you?" he whispered. "You want to wake everyone?"

He raised one hand to feel the blistered paint of the wooden sill, and stretched to press his palm against the attic window. It slid up easily under his hand. Lucky. He hadn't even thought it might be locked. He threw himself inside as the pipe swung wildly and the cat meowed below.

Sam reached into his pocket for the flashlight and switched it on. He couldn't remember the last time he'd been up here. One Christmas he'd gone into Mack's room, climbed on the bed, and pulled down the attic door to peer up into the darkness. Mack had swung him off the bed, laughing. "How do you get yourself all over the place?"

Sam's flashlight threw shadows across the floor in front of him. He angled it up: jackets on hooks that looked like old men in a row, a jumble of boots crisscrossed over each other, but nothing that looked like a birthday present.

He tiptoed across the room; Mack was sleeping just below. Under the window was another box. Ah, maybe—

Mack's presents were the best. But the box was metal and locked, too old to be interesting. He leaned over anyway, and spotted a newspaper clipping sticking out of the edge. He tugged at it but saw that it would rip before it came loose.

He crouched down: large black letters on top, a picture of a boy underneath. The nubby sweater with the zipper down the front looked familiar.

5

He caught his breath. He was the boy, but so much younger.

Such a little kid in the picture, three years old maybe. Why was he in the newspaper?

He ran his fingers over the words. He couldn't read most of them. It was a pain, not being able to read. More than a pain. But actually, the top word was easy: the *ing* stood out at the end—hadn't Mrs. Waring in the Resource Room told them a hundred times to look for groups like that? And the beginning, easy to sound: *Miss*—

Missing.

He'd been missing?

Under the picture was his name: Sam. He realized he'd been holding his breath, and let it out in a rush. The last name was Bell. Sam Bell.

Such an easy word, an easy name, but not his. Not MacKenzie.

Suddenly he was cold, so cold up there with the open window in back of him, and the early-April wind blowing in against his shoulders.

There had to be a mistake. He'd know if he'd been missing, even as a little kid, wouldn't he? He searched around in his mind, trying to remember something, anything, and then, so clearly he could almost see it, there was a room with other children, one of them a boy, flapping his hands, wanting something that belonged to Sam. Sam had clung to the toy, holding on and holding on until—

Until what?

Another memory: churning water, Night Cat on the edge of a boat, back arched, soaked, and the sound of foghorns.

Where had that come from?

Sam stood up, mouth dry, heart pounding. He heard the creak of Mack's bed underneath, and didn't move until everything was still.

He had to go back down the side of the building. He went out the attic window and grabbed the freezing pipe, sliding faster than he meant to. The pipe rattled, shook, screws popped. He went past his window, trying to stop, but couldn't, not until he reached the ground. His feet hit the dirt underneath hard enough to jar his teeth, leaving the faint taste of blood in his mouth.

Head down, shoulders hunched, he went around to the front, passing the restaurant on the end of the building, then the deli. The parking lot was empty except for Mack's pickup truck, Anima's small blue Toyota, and Onji's van with a picture of a guy taking a bite out of a hero sandwich. Night Cat was waiting at the door.

Sam fumbled in his jacket pocket for the key and went into the furniture repair shop, the cat padding silently behind him.

He walked through the workroom, threading his way around the tables. Cedar shavings crackled under his feet. Ordinarily he loved the smell of cedar, the feeling of the wood, loved the workroom, and loved Mack, who'd taught him how to cut, and join, and smooth. Mack, who'd helped him finish the birdhouses out back with their pointy roofs, and that bench down by the water for Anima.

But—missing?

Sam Bell?

Maybe he'd even been kidnapped?

By Mack? And maybe Mack wasn't even his grandfather?

Ridiculous. Why would Mack want to kidnap a kid who had trouble with reading right from the start? A kid who was into everything, breaking things? "A klutzy kid," Anima always said, smiling.

But maybe Mack hadn't realized Sam would turn out like this?

And suppose he really was missing? Suppose he didn't belong here?

Standing at the worktable Mack had set up for him years ago, he ran his hands over the scarred wood, seeing Mack's hands on his as he carved a wooden sign to hang over the table. Mack had helped him with the words, SAM'S PLACE. Mack nodding, smiling, saying, "Yes, that's the way."

What would he do without Mack?

He didn't want to be anywhere else but this place with Mack, with Onji in the deli, and Anima with her rope of hair, her hands on his shoulders, laughing. He thought of his bedroom upstairs, the river out back, the small boat in the shed.

The article was a mistake. Or he'd misunderstood. Of course, a mistake.

He'd go right upstairs now and wake Mack, ask—

But suppose it was true, and he had to go back to wherever he came from, to some strange place?

No, he'd just forget about the whole thing.

He hesitated. What about his picture? *Missing*. That was what the newspaper clipping had said, and he had to believe it.

And what about that name? He whispered it, *Sam Bell*, trying to make it fit, a name he'd never heard before.

It was a name he had to find out about. Somehow.

Sam's Dream

He was caught. Caught in eleven.
And someone was banging the doors.
Banging them open.
Banging them closed.
Footsteps coming after him.
"Sam," a voice shouted. "Where are you?"

2
Caroline

Up in front of the classroom, Mrs. Stanek was writing on the board, her raised arm tight in her purple sleeve. The chalk was thick and dusty, the words a bunch of loops and whorls that seemed to jump as Sam looked at them.

Never mind, he knew what it was all about anyway: the unit on the Middle Ages they were starting.

"*Pease porridge hot,*" Mrs. Stanek said over her shoulder. "Remember that old nursery rhyme?"

Some of the kids joined in. "*Pease porridge cold. Pease porridge in the pot, nine days old.*"

"It's what they ate in those days," genius Marcy Albert said. "Peas on thick bread shaped into plates."

"You're right," said Mrs. Stanek. "The plates were called

trenchers. After the rich ate the peas, they gave the bread away to the poor."

Across the room, Eric caught Sam's eye. He made gagging motions with his finger to his mouth.

Sam grinned; he shaded his eyes with his hands so Mrs. Stanek wouldn't notice him glancing around. She was talking about spices now, something about people using cinnamon and cloves in the medieval days. But he was hardly thinking about mashed-up peas and bread, or spices. He had to single someone out to help him read that paper in the attic, to go through the things that might be in the box. The boys would think he was weird, so it had to be a girl.

Marcy Albert was possible. She could read, but she could talk, too. He could almost hear her. *We sneaked up to his attic, can you imagine, he's looking for something but he doesn't even know exactly what.* Besides, Marcy Albert wouldn't climb up the side of the building in a million years.

There wasn't anyone else he could think of except maybe that new girl, Caroline. She'd arrived a month or so ago, the door banging open in the middle of the morning. A Kleenex coiled out of her sleeve like a white snake; her hair was tangerine. Nice face, ski-jump nose, freckles, tinted glasses.

Since then all she'd done was read every chance she had, a dozen bracelets jangling as she turned the pages. She wasn't too friendly; he hadn't seen her smile once.

Now Mrs. Stanek marched around the room. "Ah,

Sam." She put a picture of a castle on his desk. "Maybe you could make one for us. There's cardboard in the closet, paper, scissors, glue—"

Nice going, Mrs. Stanek, he wanted to say; she knew he wouldn't have to read a word to cut out a castle.

"We'll have a lovely feast at the end of the unit," Mrs. Stanek said as she kept moving.

With peas on bread?

Sam looked over at Eric and slashed his throat with one finger. Eric slashed back. Mrs. Stanek raised her eyebrows, and Eric turned the throat slashing into throat scratching.

Sam almost laughed, but he thought of the attic again, and reading the clipping. He glanced over at the new girl, her head bent over her book.

Lunchtime came. "We're all friends in fifth grade," Mrs. Stanek said, as she always did. That meant everyone had to sit in the cafeteria the way they lined up. She never noticed the switching around on the stairs, kids sliding along the banisters, using their elbows to get where they wanted. But no one had elbows as sharp as his. By the last turn, he was in back of Caroline New Girl, and managed to slide onto the bench next to her.

He opened his lunch bag, feeling the sun that gleamed in from the high windows overhead. He glanced at her: the lunch bag on her lap, the book on the table in front of her. She began to turn the pages, reaching into the bag for a sandwich.

He cleared his throat. "I'm Sam." Dumb, she had to know that by now.

The ends of her sandwich were ragged, the crusts torn off. It looked as if the whole thing had been glued together with purple jelly.

Sam didn't know what his own lunch was yet. Every morning he stopped at Onji's Deli next door and had a second breakfast in the warm back room while Onji made a sandwich, a meatball hero maybe, or turkey on thick slabs of rye bread. Best lunch in the school. Sam unwrapped today's, pastrami with sauerkraut on rye, a couple of pickles in a Baggie, and a bunch of salty pretzel sticks.

He knew she was looking at him. Maybe he should ask if she wanted some, but already she'd taken a huge bite of hers, jelly dripping onto her sweater. And she was smiling a little, bread on her braces. Nice smile.

She pointed with a jelly-tipped finger.

He looked down: a Gummi Bear poked out of his sandwich. That Onji!

"There are more of them in with the pickles," she said as if she might laugh.

He picked them out. Eleven of them. "It's my birthday, but don't tell anyone. Mrs. Stanek will make me wear that crown thing."

She grinned again. "So, Sam."

"Yeah."

"Sam as in *Sam I Am?* As in *My Brother Sam Is Dead?*

Samuel Morse, *Sam and the Firefly*? Maybe Sam Spade, the detective?"

He knew them all from books Anima had read to him. "Samson."

"Samson was tough."

"I'm tougher, but don't tell anyone that, either."

"I'm a sphinx." A quick smile and she swiped at a blob of jelly at the corner of her mouth, her bracelets clinking. "Sam what, again?"

"MacKenzie." Something lurched in his chest. *Bell*.

"Hey, Sam MacKenzie, birthday kid, slide over one of those Gummi Bears. Just one won't kill my braces."

She was the one. Somehow he'd get her to help. He grinned at her and handed her a couple.

"One thing." She looked up at the windows the way he'd done. "Don't think I'm going to be friends. I won't be here long enough."

He sat there chewing, pretending he didn't care whether she was his friend or not. The lunch hour seemed endless, but at last they went back to the classroom to work on the medieval project.

He glanced up at the clock: a half hour before he had to go to Mrs. Waring's Resource Room.

Five kids were writing a play, and Eric was jumping around in front with a sword.

"Calm down." Mrs. Stanek went around the room. She stopped at Sam's desk. "I have another picture of a castle for you."

Sam looked at it: fields, a knight in armor, and a dark castle in the mist with turrets, and a moat, and slits for windows. A castle so dark you could hardly see to copy it. He held it up. Something was wrong with it. He'd seen a castle once somewhere, and it didn't look much like this.

"All right?" Mrs. Stanek asked.

"Nothing to it." Impossible with cardboard.

"Need some help?"

He shook his head. But Mrs. Stanek snapped her fingers. "Caroline—"

"A girl?" He curled his lip.

"We're all friends in fifth grade. Caroline?"

Caroline blinked, her eyebrows a V over her forehead.

"I'd like you to work on the castle project with Sam." Mrs. Stanek smiled at them with large teeth, as if she were doing them a favor.

Caroline closed her book. She screeched her desk over a few feet, Kleenex floating out behind her.

"You might keep a diary of your progress," Mrs. Stanek told her as she moved toward another group. "Write down the steps you take."

Caroline rummaged around inside her desk and pulled out a lipstick.

A lipstick?

She ran it over her mouth, smacking her lips, then smeared most of it away with the back of her hand.

"How old are you, anyway?" he asked.

"Ten years, eight months"—she screwed up her face with its dots of freckles—"and nine days. Or so."

"You left about ten years, eight months, and—"

"Nine days?"

"—worth of Kleenex on the floor, and you have lipstick on your braces."

"Whatever."

"That's what I say." This kid was terrific. He kept his mouth still. No smile. Not friends.

She picked up the picture of the castle, turning it one way and then another. "Who knows what this is about?" But then she stood one of the cardboard pieces he'd found in the closet on end and made cutting motions. "I guess we could cut squares into the top and glue the whole mess together."

As he looked at her, the idea came to him. Suppose they built a castle out of wood? It wouldn't have to be much, just four slabs knocked together. And then maybe—

"My grandfather has a workshop. We could build a wooden one there," he said, almost as if he didn't care one way or the other.

And read what was up in the attic. He'd fix the pipe, or maybe Mack would be out and they'd use the pull-down stairs.

"Not work in the classroom?" she said.

"Well, some of it, I guess." He glanced up toward Mrs. Stanek, who was watching them, looking pleased. "I don't think she'd mind."

"One thing. Where do you live?"

"One thing." He echoed her words, for fun. "It's on the road out of town. We'll take the school bus."

"But how will I get home again? I live near the school."

"A town bus goes along the road. Don't worry—"

"I can come on Wednesday, or maybe Friday." She hesitated. "I have to babysit for my little sister sometimes."

"Wednesday's good. Friday's good."

Possible. Anything was possible.

Caroline's fingers went to her hair, twirling a piece in front. "Maybe."

He grinned. "Yes."

3
Sam's Birthday

Mack brought out the crocheted tablecloth that he kept for special occasions, a web of a cloth that had belonged to Sam's grandmother Lydia, dead before he was born. Some of the holes were meant to be there, a pattern of stars; others Sam had poked in when he was five, to surprise Mack.

Had Lydia really been his grandmother?

Sam helped put out the plates, taking quick looks at Mack. He'd thought about Mack all day. When he was five or six, he'd lean his head back to see Mack's blue eyes crinkling, the lines around them deepening, convinced that Mack was a giant; Mack could do anything, even though he limped sometimes, bending to rub his leg. Lately flecks of gray were coming into his dark hair and beard, and Onji would nudge Sam: "Your grandfather's getting to be an old guy." Onji, who had only a fringe of hair around the edges.

Mack was quiet, and that was fine with Sam. They spent hours in the workroom, Mack humming, with just a word here or there: *"Onji's cooking roast beef in the deli, smells good. . . . A hawk's circling above the river. . . ."* Mack running his hands over a shelf Sam had finished: *"I couldn't have done better."*

Could it be that Mack wasn't his grandfather? But didn't everyone say they looked alike, even though Sam was bone thin? A walking skeleton, Onji said, a Halloween costume. Sam touched his nose, ran his fingers over his mouth. How could he tell if his face was really like Mack's?

And hadn't Mack showed him a picture of his parents, Julia and Luke? He had no memory of either of them; both had died, his father in the army, Mack had told him, and Julia from a heart problem.

Just before dark, Anima came upstairs to their apartment from her restaurant, her dark shiny braid bouncing on her back. Her arms were filled with trays of food. "Ah, please take these, Mack. Watch, they're hot."

Anima's voice was clear and high, laughter always just behind her words. She touched Sam's shoulder. "How's my boy?" She moved lightly, like one of the small yellow finches that flew by every fall. The sari she wore tonight was yellow too, floating behind her.

"Beef curry because it's your favorite, Sam," she said, a little breathless. "So spicy you'll taste it on your tongue until bedtime. And chicken korma for Mack with lots of coconut milk." She winked at Sam. "I have to be nice to him until he finishes making the cabinet for the restaurant."

Mack looked up at the ceiling, his eyes crinkling. "And after that you want shelves in the hallway, a bookcase for your living room—"

"All the chicken you want forever," she said.

Sam looked from one to the other. Did Anima know about him?

She helped them set everything out, talking about the cabinet, which would have glass doors and carved feet. She glanced at him. "Quiet tonight, Sam?"

Before he could answer, heavy footsteps came up the stairs, and Onji filled the kitchen, carrying a huge chocolate birthday cake that had SAM scrawled across the top. All of Onji was wide and round, his face, his nose, even his thick ears that looked as if they'd been stuck on the side of his head like blobs of clay.

Onji clamped his hand on Sam's shoulder: "Eleven years old, this skinny little kid. Who could believe it?"

"Some cake, Onji! Thanks."

Mack nodded. "That's a pretty good-looking cake for a guy who does nothing but slice roast beef all day."

"Not bad at all," Anima said.

"Believe it," Onji said, setting the cake on the counter.

Sam knew they were waiting for him to slide his finger around the edge of the plate and scoop up a dab of icing. He reached out and took a mouthful of the sweet chocolate. "Terrific."

23

He looked at the three of them, and then at the table with its cloth as they sat down. The paneled kitchen was always cozy, with flames from the fireplace casting orange light over them, but now everything seemed strange, almost as if he didn't belong.

Sam had dreamed of another kitchen last night, white, cold. He'd reached for an apple on the counter, and a woman had come toward him, her arm raised. Night Cat had darted under the table, and Sam had backed up against the huge refrigerator, terrified.

Concentrate on dinner, on now, he told himself. *Think about the birthday cake that Onji covered with candles.* He caught the word *pipe.*

Onji looked at Sam from under bushy eyebrows. "It's falling off the side of the wall, banging back and forth."

Everyone was looking at him.

"Last week he lost an oar," Onji said. "The week before, the shed door was off its hinges."

Onji was teasing, and Mack and Anima were laughing, but Sam couldn't stop himself. "Not me," he said. "I didn't touch the pipe."

"You sure?" Onji grinned.

"Sure I'm sure."

It was too late to take the lie back, too late to say yes, he'd been up at night, up in that attic, and to please tell him what that clipping was all about.

"For the first time," Anima said, "we found a perfect place to hide your presents."

Mack stood up and opened the oven door. He turned to Sam, smiling.

"Fooled you this time." Anima's teeth were white against her warm dark skin.

If only he'd looked in the oven. He never would have gone up to the attic, never would have known about the clipping, never would have had to find out more.

Anima handed him a square package wrapped in blue paper. "Wait, I have to tell you—" She leaned over him. "It's a book but you won't have much to read."

He tore the paper away and opened it to see drawings, patterns, measurements: dozens of wood projects, and very few words. He looked up at her. "You're the best, Anima."

She smiled. "Banana crepes later in my apartment." Her favorites. She'd learned to make them as a child in Kerala, and told him once that her mother's recipe book was one of the few things she'd brought to America with her.

"But wait," Onji said, putting a bag in front of Sam. "Here comes a terrific present." Mack and Anima were laughing again.

"Not one of those T-shirts." Sam held it up. It was a blinding yellow, miles too big, ONJI'S DELI—MEAT AND MORE spelled out in green.

"You'll grow into it," Onji said.

Sam laughed too, feeling better. The clipping in the attic had to be a mistake.

Mack took the last package out of the oven and put it on

the table. "Heavy," he said, and Sam could see how pleased he was about it.

Under the paper was a second wrapping of flannel. Sam pulled the cloth away and sat back to look at his present. It was much older than he was, older even than Mack, and the handle was worn from years of use: a plane, a tool to smooth wood.

Sam rested his hand on the knob that would move almost by itself. It would take only a little pressure to run the bottom of the plane across the wood, to curl the roughness away from whatever he was making, until the wood felt like satin.

"It was my father's." Mack spread his hands wide. "You're old enough, you deserve it."

Sam looked across the table; it was a wonderful thing to have, to add to the tools on his worktable, but even more special because it had been in his family. *His family?* His grandfather? His great-grandfather?

He reached out to hug Mack. *Please let things be the same.*

It didn't take long to finish dinner. Mack lighted the candles on the cake. "He's only eleven, Onji," he said. "There must be thirty here."

Onji ran his hand over his bald head. "Thirty-three." He turned to Sam. "Mack can't count very well. Three for every year." He looked up at the ceiling as Mack and Anima laughed. "Is that right? Yes."

They sang "Happy Birthday," and afterward Anima said, "If Night Cat could sing, he'd sound like Mack and Onji."

"Better," Sam said. He blew out the candles, and everything did seem the same: all of them smiling at him, the taste of the cake, the presents.

They hurried to put the plates in the dishwasher. It was time for them to go to Anima's. They walked through her restaurant, where small yellow flowers in baskets decorated the tables. Anima stopped to say hello to people, to nod at the waiters, and then they went upstairs to her living room, as they had almost every night since they found out Sam had trouble reading.

He remembered it vaguely, the beginning of her reading to them. He pictured himself sitting on Anima's couch, Mack next to him, Anima opposite, and Onji coming up the stairs. "Sam has to know the world," Anima had said. "If he can't read yet, one thing we can do while we try to help him is to give him the world of books."

Mack had nodded.

And Onji: "How?"

"I'll read aloud every night." So when things quieted in the restaurant, Anima read to all of them for at least an hour. And what she read! Long poems, the Bible, stories about a kid who dug holes, about a spider who saved a pig. Anima's accent made her sound like an English queen.

Sometimes they loved what she read, and sometimes they didn't. She'd shrug, reading about copper mining or sea routes. Onji would fall asleep, his snores almost drowning her out. And sometimes Mack put his head back, his eyes closed. But Sam never slept.

Tonight Anima began an Iroquois legend as they ate the crepes that had been made downstairs in the restaurant. Mack shook his head; he must have heard this one before. He reached out with one hand as if he'd stop her.

But Anima kept going. "The Creator promised land to the people if they'd stop fighting. They tried, but the arguing began again. Angry, God scooped up the land to carry it back to the sky. But ah! It fell and broke into a thousand pieces, some so small you could get your arms around them. They became islands, floating in a river so large it was almost an ocean."

Sam knew that story; someone had told it to him long ago. And somehow, he remembered that river, too.

Sam's Dream

Cold. Freezing.
Going so fast he couldn't catch his breath.
Skimming over the water, spray on his face, in his eyes.
Breathing through his mouth, the in-and-out sound of it echoing
in his ears, Night Cat there beside him.
The water was dark and wide. Huge chunks of ice spun
beneath him, crashing into each other.
A house flashed by in the water, its windows black and shiny,
and then a flag on a mound of earth, whipping against a pole.
High up over his head, a number, eleven.
He put his arms up and covered his face.

4
The River

Saturday, no school. Free.

The wind roughed the river up into small curls, but for the first time this spring the sun was almost hot on Sam's head and shoulders.

He pulled the rowboat out of the shed, a huge shed big enough for five rowboats, and dragged it across the grass, breathing in the smell of the clean water at the river's edge.

Mack slid open the back window of the workshop, a level in his hand. "Be careful, Sam."

And from the deli window next door, Onji called, "He's the only kid who could drown himself in six inches of water."

"Don't worry," Sam called back. He knew what Mack was thinking. Last week Sam had rowed past the bridge where the river widened out, the water deeper and swifter there. Somehow one of his oars had floated away from the boat, leaving him a mile downriver to wait for someone to pull him and the boat onto the bank.

"Stay this side of the bridge. All right?"

"I will."

"He's an accident waiting to happen," Onji said.

Mack nodded. "Can't take your eyes off him for two seconds."

They were joking, but Sam knew Mack was afraid of the water. Sam threw his sneakers into the boat, peeled off his socks, and splashed his way into the water.

The temperature was shocking, numbing his toes. He pushed the boat hard, scraping the bottom along the sand, grit under his feet, and jumped in, rubbing his feet with cold hands.

Night Cat came to the edge of the water and meowed. Not asking. Ordering.

Sam angled back and scooped him up. "Okay?" He buried his face in the cat's fur. It had a smell all its own, a Night Cat smell. There was that wisp of a memory: the cat, fur matted down, teetering on the edge of a boat. And Sam, reaching, reaching, the boat tilting, the edge almost level with the water.

He felt a pulse in his throat, his heart thumping, as Night Cat twisted away from him and darted to the backseat.

Stop, he told himself.

The pipe clanked against the building. He stared at it. It was worse every day. How was he going to get Caroline up to the attic? Sometimes Mack went away for an hour or two to deliver furniture, but he couldn't count on it. Was it possible to screw the pipe back to the side of the wall?

But Onji saw too much; Onji saw almost everything. Sam would just have to wait and see.

He waved back at both windows, a little guilty that he wasn't helping Onji today. Saturday was Onji's busy day. And Mack's, too. Mack had been in the workroom early, repairing an old chair, smoothing out a deep gash in one of the legs and threading in new caning for the seat.

Sam began to row, feeling the pull in his arms and his back. As the boat moved away from the shore, the sound of Indian music floated out of Anima's restaurant, light music with bells that reminded him of Anima herself.

Sam rowed fast, through the narrow channel where the rushes were over his head. He pulled the dripping oars into the boat and dropped the anchor, a brick tied with a rope, onto the sandy bottom.

Overhead, the stalks swayed and rattled against each other, and a kingfisher flew up and away from him. He sat back and raised his face to the sun, listening to the water lapping against the boat.

It was the best place to think.

Missing. He said it aloud, and Night Cat looked up at him. "I have to think about all this, figure out . . ." His voice trailed off.

Mack always tackled things in steps, counting on his fingers, one of them bent from a long-ago accident. "First sand the pieces, then join them with carpenter's glue, use the clamps until everything dries. Next, sand again, stain—"

And Mrs. Waring in the Resource Room: "Look at the syllables, break the word down, one piece after another."

Steps.

All right.

Caroline first. She was the key. They'd open the box somehow, she'd read what the clipping said, and anything else that might be there.

Caroline didn't know he could hardly read. With her head down, turning pages, she might not have noticed that he left for the Resource Room every afternoon.

How could he tell her?

His mind veered off. That room. He knew it as well as Mack's workshop. And Mrs. Waring, the smell of her lunch coffee strong as she spoke, her voice with a twang: *Saaam*. Her smile was great, even though her teeth were a little crooked.

Once she'd showed him a book with about four words on each page, words he couldn't read. "What does it all look like to you?" she'd asked.

He'd shrugged. How could he say the lines moved like black spiders, stretching their legs and waving their feelers across the pages?

She was sorry, he could see that. "Look." She pointed out the window. "What do you see?"

"Trees, two of them."

"Yes. You see the branches, the leaves. And that tells you they're not houses, or clouds. You don't even have to think about it. Trees."

He'd felt something begin in his chest, because he couldn't imagine that happening when he read.

"That's the way it is with words," she'd said. "After a while, the circles and lines will mean things. They'll jump out at you, so that trees are trees, and not clouds."

The bell had rung then, and he'd escaped. That thing in his chest was growing, was going to explode. He'd held it in while they gathered up their books in the classroom, held it in on the bus, almost bursting with it, just waiting until he reached Mack in the workshop.

Mack had sat with him on the bench at the side wall as it finally burst out into the loud sound of his crying. Mack's arm had gone around him, and he'd hardly been able to get the words out, only "—spiders on the page that will never look like anything but spiders."

He'd buried his head in Mack's shirt, smelling furniture wax and pine, and Mack had cleared his throat. "You have a gift, Sam. A gift like mine."

He'd burrowed deeper into Mack's shirt, listening.

"You don't know it yet," Mack had said, "but it's the wood. It talks to us."

What did that have to do with anything?

"Already you feel the wood under your fingers. I've seen you."

That was true. Sam would run his fingers over the wood, imagining where it had come from: pine from the forests here in New York State, or mahogany from the jungles far away. He knew what the woods were good for, what they could be made into.

"You read the wood," Mack had said. "And that's something that almost no one else can do."

Mack had turned up Sam's chin with those broad fingers. "You'll learn to read, Sam. It may take longer than most, it may never be your strong point. But you have this." Mack's hand swept over the workroom, wood stacked waiting to become chairs or tables, tools gleaming. And in a voice Sam strained to hear: "You have me, Sam. Me, and Onji, and Anima. And we all love you more than anything."

Now clouds moved between the sun and the boat. Sam pulled his jacket up against his neck, and Night Cat slid off the backseat, almost as if he didn't have bones, and curled up next to him.

Sam didn't think in steps. He'd started out thinking about telling Caroline, and instead he was remembering Mack that day long ago. No wonder he mixed up those syllables, those words. "But I read the wood," he told Night Cat, and felt better until he thought again about being missing.

He pulled the oars out, one old and dark, the other fresh wood. He and Mack had cut the new oar and sanded it just the other day.

Mack, Onji, and Anima. Did all three know about that

newspaper clipping? And even though he'd never ask straight out, he'd have to begin in steps to find out where he'd come from, even though he wasn't sure what he'd do when he knew.

One thing, as Caroline would say. He'd never be happy anywhere else.

5
Beginning

Sometimes Sam took a detour on the way to Mrs. Waring's Resource Room. He'd open the side door, stick a book in the edge so it wouldn't lock behind him, and sit outside to breathe in a little air.

Or maybe he'd slide along the corridor and have a gargling contest at the fountain with Robert, who came to the Resource Room from the opposite direction.

It was a little dangerous because Mr. Ramon, the assistant principal, patrolled the halls.

This afternoon, Sam hadn't gotten three steps away from the classroom when Caroline opened the door. "Going to the Media Center?"

He stopped. He hadn't told her about his reading yet,

and she was coming home with him this afternoon. "Want to go outside?" he asked.

"I guess." She followed him out. The grass was coming in green now, and a robin chirped in one of the two trees Mrs. Waring had pointed out years ago.

Sam sank down on the step, and Caroline sat too. "One thing? Are we allowed to do this?" she asked, pulling her hair into a knot in back of her head.

He laughed. "One thing? No."

She waved her hand. She was wearing nail polish, a horrible Easter egg purple. "You do this every afternoon after lunch." Her eyes were wide behind her glasses. "What nerve."

So she'd noticed. "Most of the time I go to the Resource Room for reading," he said.

She reached out to touch one of the daffodils at the side of the steps. He couldn't see her face.

"I have a little trouble reading." A *little?* "They call it a learning disability. I'm supposed to spend part of the day in a regular classroom and part in the Resource Room." He rushed on. "When you come over to work on the castle, I could use some help."

"I've never taught anyone to read, but I suppose I could try."

It made him grin to think about it: Caroline trying to teach him how to read. Everyone else had tried, and kept trying; they didn't want to admit that he'd given up.

Anima read aloud every night, running her fingers along the words so he could see. Mack cut cards with pictures and the words underneath. He pulled them out as often as he could and made Sam try to read them. And even Onji had taped up signs along the salad bar. *"Macaroni, Sam, for Pete's sake. What else could it be?"* as Anima had said gently, *"Onji, I don't think you spell* macaroni *with a* y.*"*

They'd all laughed, and Onji had winked. "So I don't spell too well, Sam."

Now Sam began again. "There's a box in the attic." He waved his hand. "Maybe you'd read some stuff to me."

"What kind of stuff?"

"A newspaper clipping with my picture, to begin with. It says I was missing. Am missing?" He hesitated. "Still missing?"

Caroline peered at him, her glasses in her lap now. "You're joking."

He shook his head. "I wish."

"I'll try." She hesitated. "But listen, I don't have much time."

What had she told him the other day in the cafeteria? *"Don't think I'm going to be friends. I won't be here long enough."*

"I'm leaving for my own castle soon," she said.

"You're joking now."

"You don't think I look like a princess?" She grinned, showing her braces. There was a constellation of freckles on her cheeks. "I'm leaving, but not for a castle."

"But—"

"My father's a painter, so we have to go where he wants to paint."

Sam raised his shoulders. "He could paint right here. There are a million houses, I bet."

She laughed. "He paints sunsets, and waves crashing on the shore, and rain on the water." She waved her hand, bracelets jangling. "Stuff like that. My mother makes figures out of clay." She raised one shoulder. "I can't draw a straight line."

Sam nodded.

"We move around. Last winter we were in California, and the spring in Canada. I've never even been in New York State before." She spread her hands wide. "My father's friend lent us a house until we go somewhere else. A place called Turnerville."

He didn't want her to know how sorry he was, so he just said, "Turnerville."

"It's still in New York, I think." The bracelets jangled again.

"How can you do that? Keep moving around—" But then he stopped. It wasn't the first time kids had come for only a couple of months. That Chinese kid whose father did something with computers left after a year, and sent a pack of pictures to the class. A girl, he couldn't remember her name, whose mother was going to college somewhere nearby. They'd left too. And the kids whose families came to pick apples and grapes—

The outside door opened behind them. "I can't believe this. You two out here getting a tan."

Mr. Ramon.

"I'll give you two minutes to get where you're supposed to be."

They stood up. Sam could see that Caroline's face was red. She probably wasn't used to getting into trouble the way he was.

He slid into Mrs. Waring's room, late again, spreading his hands wide. "Sorry, I was just . . ." He let his voice trail off as Mrs. Waring shook her head.

He opened his book, feeling good. Mr. Ramon had let them go without detention. But more than that, Caroline knew about the reading and didn't mind. And even if she had to leave soon, they still had time. She wasn't moving tomorrow, after all.

6
Going Home

When the bell rang, they climbed on the bus. Sam marched past the empty seat next to Caroline and went to the back. He and Eric sat together every day and he'd have heard about it if he'd sat with her. "A *girl, MacKenzie?*"

He swung into the seat, giving Eric a light dig in the ribs with his elbow. In back of them Joseph leaned forward with Life Savers. Sam sat, crunching candy, until his stop, then went down the aisle and out the door. He walked two or three steps before he turned, but Caroline wasn't there. She hadn't gotten off the bus.

He watched it rumble away, but the door opened at the next stop. A kid came down the steps, and then Caroline. "I was reading," she called, and walked toward him.

Mack's truck was in the parking lot. Sam stopped; he'd

been sure Mack was going to deliver furniture today. If Mack was home, how could they get into the attic? He shook his head. He'd been counting on it.

Inside the workroom, Mack was nowhere in sight, but a bowl of fruit and nuts from Anima was on the counter, and cupcakes that Onji's daughter, Ellie, had brought last night.

Mack had left water bottles for them, and paper napkins folded carefully.

Sam watched Caroline as she glanced around, her fingers tapping her lips. The sign, SAM'S PLACE, hung over his table. A dresser, newly glued together, clamped and turned on its side, gave off the smell of polish. The open window framed the river so the water with its reeds and birds seemed part of the room, and the chatter of jays was loud as a hawk circled overhead.

Caroline reached absently for a piece of fruit. "This is the best place I've ever been."

Her words fizzed inside him, almost like the fizzy water he was drinking. He knew she could see it in his face. He grinned and motioned to a bench. "Sit there, I want to see where Mack is."

He went to the stairs and called. Mack wasn't upstairs, but not far, probably at Onji's, having coffee.

Caroline hadn't moved from the window. "There are Canadian geese out there, a pair of them," she said. "So where's the stuff you wanted me to read? The stuff about your being missing?"

He raised his shoulders, hoping she couldn't see how

disappointed he was. "Shhh," he said. "Not today. We have to wait until Mack delivers furniture."

Her face fell. "I've been thinking about it." She pushed at her sleeves. "We have to start the castle, anyway."

"Right." Large pieces of plywood were stacked in a bin under the tools. He dragged a few to his worktable as she watched.

"Can you do this?" she asked.

"Cut? Yep. Smooth out the pieces and join them."

She pulled out a small green notebook. "I brought this for the journal. Remember, Mrs. Stanek said—"

He nodded. "First write in 'plywood, pieces of wood layered onto each other.' " He knew he was talking to impress her. "It's easy to work with. But you have to be careful cutting it." He'd hurt himself dozens of times on the edges of wood like this.

"I'll mark that down." She ran her hand over the edges. "Great, a splinter already. But it could be worse."

"Wait till we start using the saw," he said.

Next door, Onji began to sing. His voice was loud, off-key, and Mack chimed in, his voice deeper, surer. It was an old song, something about blue skies, or gray skies, and they stopped after a minute, laughing.

Caroline sucked on her finger. "Who's that?"

"Onji in the deli next door and my grandfather Mack. They sing sometimes. Anima says they hurt her ears."

"Who's—"

"Anima? She owns Kerala House, the Indian restaurant

47

down at the end of the building. She reads to us, she cooks, she does everything." He spread his hands. "You'll like Anima. You'll like all of them."

Caroline held up her finger. "My splinter's gone. I'm going to live. So let's talk about *missing* for a minute."

He hesitated. "I don't know. There's just that clipping, and I was only about three."

"Still—" She touched her forehead. "Everything that happens to you is up there. You just have to pull it out."

"Anima says something like that," he said. "Your brain is a computer. Touch the right button and everything will come spewing out."

He smiled, reminded that Anima would make a face. *"Trouble is,"* she'd say, *"I can't find the button."*

Caroline looked out the window again as she spoke. "I remember a lot from when I was a little kid. My father holding me up, showing me his painting." A flash of her braces. "I thought the sun was an egg."

She leaned forward. "The day my sister, Denise, was born. My mother let me give her a second name. I picked Emma." Her voice was low. "I remember moving from school to school, walking in the classroom in the middle of the term, everyone looking at me, feeling so—"

She didn't finish, but Sam knew she meant *bad*, or *terrible*. What would it be like to go from place to place, school to school, never having time to make friends?

But she was on tiptoes now, watching something

outside. "What do you remember?" she asked. "There must be something up there in your brain."

"Maybe." He hesitated. "The sweater in the newspaper clipping."

She was still, listening.

"Anima might have it." He tried to remember. "I was helping her once and I saw it in a drawer. It was a mess." He pictured Anima's small hands going to it, smoothing the matted wool.

But then Mack stood in the doorway, smiling at them. He had a great look to him, Sam thought, a kind look, with his eyes crinkling. "Hi, you two, and glad you're here, Caroline," he said. "Everything all right?"

They nodded.

"I have a few things to do in the kitchen." He tapped the edge of the door and went upstairs.

Sam shook his head at Caroline, warning her not to say anything else.

"Why don't you just ask him about it?" she whispered.

He leaned closer. "I lied about being up there. I don't want him to know. But it's more than that. It's been a secret. If he finds out I know about this, won't everything be different? Suppose I belong somewhere else?" He listened to Mack's footsteps overhead, and pointed up. "Shhh."

"All right. The castle, then." She waggled her hands back and forth. "How are we going to do this?"

He nodded. *Think about the castle, not the sweater and*

where it came from. "If the castle's too small, it'll look like nothing. Too big and it'll look—close." That wasn't the right word. "We want it to seem far away." *Shrouded in mist.* That felt like something Anima might have read aloud.

He began to draw on a piece of paper to show Caroline what he meant. He tried to make it like the pictures they'd seen. A tower, turrets, the castle narrower than it was high so it would seem taller.

Sam pointed to the plywood on the table. "Can you draw the lines? We'll mark in the turrets before we cut." He swept the air with his hands. "And draw doors, round on top—"

Caroline's eyes were closed. "It'll be a place you'd want to live, inside forever, never moving away."

He gave her a pencil and a ruler, then sat back as she drew, watching her rub out mistakes with her thumb.

He just wanted to live here, right here, and nowhere else.

7
The Attic

On Friday Mack unclamped the dresser, loaded it on the truck, and drove off. Sam and Caroline were in the workroom alone. "We have to watch for customers," Sam told her. "But there might not be anyone. We'll wait a few minutes, then we'll go up to the attic."

He felt a catch in his throat. It was going to happen this afternoon; it was going to happen now.

Mack had a collection of keys, dozens of them on a metal ring in the junk drawer, and another hefty pile in one of the cabinets. "I need a small key. Something that will fit that locked box."

He sifted through both sets. Most of the keys were large, front door keys or ornate iron keys that Mack used to open antique dressers he bought and repaired, then sold at auctions.

Caroline gathered up the few small keys he found, and they went upstairs to Mack's room. Everything was neat there, the carved armoire, the brushes on the dresser, and the black-and-white picture of a woman in a hat that framed her dark hair. The woman was young, but if she were alive now, she'd be his grandmother. Mack had run his fingers over the frame. *"Lydia. She'd have thought you were great, Sam."*

Sam took off his sneakers and stood on the navy blue quilt that covered the bed. He reached for the rope to pull down the door with its stairway attached. It was heavy and swung down slowly.

He climbed the steps to the top, then crouched on the edge of the attic floor and reached for Caroline. She didn't take his hand. "I can do it," she said, slipping out of her sneakers too and climbing up. "I'm tough."

Tough. His own word.

In the attic, dim light came from the windows. The flashlight beamed across the floor, its light splashing a circular pattern on the far wall. There were small creaking sounds, the house settling around them. "Breathing," Caroline said.

"Mice," Sam said, to tease her.

They knelt on the floor, trying one key after another. It was stifling, even this early in the spring, and Sam wiped his face with his sleeve. But Caroline looked cool; she sat back on her heels and waited. He tried not to glance at the edge of the newspaper clipping, not yet.

None of the keys fit.

He slid down the stairs, this time to the workroom for a hammer and a screwdriver.

Onji came in the back door. "I thought the girl was here."

Sam swallowed. "Yes."

Onji looked around. "Where did she get herself to?"

Sam couldn't imagine what to say, but before he could open his mouth, Onji was talking again. "Anyway, why don't you guys come over for a soda, or some cocoa?"

Sam nodded. "If there's time later, all right?" He waited until Onji went back out the door, listening to his heavy footsteps on the path.

Sam took the tools up to Mack's room, checking the window to be sure the truck was still gone. Onji was in the parking lot, his hands on his hips. Looking for Caroline? But Ellie's car pulled in. It was all right.

Sam stood on Mack's bed and reached for the stair railing. Caroline was perched on the attic floor, looking down, her face almost ghostly in the half-light.

He went up the steps with the tools. "If I break the lock, I can't fix it. Mack will know if he ever comes up here."

"Up to you," Caroline said. She leaned over to pull gently at the newspaper clipping. "Most of it must be inside the box."

"Other things might be in there too." How could he stop

now? He crouched and angled the screwdriver into the top of the lock. He hit it with the hammer and missed, denting the metal. The sound was loud in his ears, and Caroline's eyes were wide.

He tried several times, until at last the lock snapped open. Not broken. They could close it again after they were finished and no one would know. They looked at each other across the box. "Ah," Caroline said.

Sam slid off the lock and pushed back the top of the box. The clipping drifted out, and underneath, papers were stacked in a pile. On top was a photo of a boat. Caroline picked it up. "A sailboat. Beautiful."

He'd know about the clipping any second. He had time to wait. He took the picture in his hand. The boat was angled away from them; its white sails matched the small whitecaps on the water. The sky in the background was so blue it almost hurt to look at it.

What would it be like to take that boat out on the water? Not a narrow branch of a river like the one out back, but wide water, deep water?

Caroline had the clipping in her hand. "Sam." She raised her eyebrows. "Bell?"

"Yes."

"Missing. Disappeared in a boating accident on Saturday."

Night Cat, wet, bedraggled, the sound of foghorns, the boat tipping so the water was almost level with the edge.

Was that it?

Caroline went on. "It was reported that the boy was seen as he went over the side of the boat, but because of the weather conditions he was not seen again." She reached out to touch his shoulder. "Oh, Sam-I-Am."

Sam, still holding the picture of the sailboat, saw that his hands were trembling. How could he feel so cold now in that warm, close attic? It was almost as if he were in that water, unable to catch his breath.

And was this the boat? *Water sloshing up over the edge, pouring in, the feel of Night Cat's fur under his fingers, then water filling his mouth, his throat.*

They stared down at the picture, the boy's dark hair, *his* hair, the zippered sweater. Sam Bell.

Caroline was reaching for the stack of papers that were held together with a rubber band when he heard the sound of a motor.

"The truck." He scrambled up. There was no time to put things back together, but in that moment he saw a small bundle of cloth in the bottom of the box, cloth that seemed familiar.

But they raced down the stairs, and slammed up the attic door so it exploded back against the ceiling. In one motion, Sam smoothed the quilt as Caroline scrambled for their sneakers. They pushed into them and raced down to the workroom, breathless, just before Mack opened the outside door.

The picture of the boat was still in Sam's hand; he slid it, facedown, onto his table.

"Hungry, you guys?" Mack asked. "Want a snack? I could go over to Onji's and get something."

"We're all right," Sam said.

"Maybe I'll just go over myself for a quick cup of coffee," Mack said.

Caroline's bus wouldn't come for another half hour. "We'll work on the castle." Sam tried to get the words out evenly as Mack left.

"And I'll write what we saw upstairs in the back of the notebook."

Sam stood looking at the door.

"We'll find it out, all of it, before I have to leave. And we'll finish the castle, too." Her voice was uncertain.

He knew she wasn't sure, and neither was he.

8
The Boat

It was dark and cold, and Sam waited for Mack to be in bed and asleep. It was close to midnight when he went out to the shed, the sound of the water lapping against the rocks in front of him. He dragged the ladder from its hook on the side wall, a poor-looking thing, missing a rung.

He leaned it against the side of the building, where it reached just a little higher than his bedroom window. He squinted up at it in the dark. Somehow he was going to get back into that attic tonight.

If he climbed up and stood on the very top of the ladder, could he reach the sill and pull himself up and inside?

He'd probably kill himself.

But the pipe was still attached to the top of the building. Maybe he could hold on to it from the ladder, not putting much weight on it, just using it for balance for the second or two he'd need it.

He wanted to carry everything back down. He tiptoed back into the workroom and found a plastic bag to take with him.

He began to climb. Night Cat was outside, his front paws on the bottom rung, looking up. "Go away," Sam whispered.

The cat meowed.

"Get down." His voice was too loud. Lights went on in Anima's apartment, and then Onji's.

Sam leaned against the wall of the building, trying not to breathe, entirely still, as the cat came up another rung, still meowing.

Onji's window opened, his head out, looking around, and then Anima's window too.

"It's the cat," Onji said.

"I'll go down," Anima said.

No moon tonight, just a glimmer of light from the water. Sam backed down the ladder—

"I heard him," Sam called up to them, hoping they'd think he was still in his bedroom. "I'll go down for him."

Onji's voice was irritable. "The cat has everyone awake."

"That cat," Anima said, but there was laughter in her voice.

How many times had they said it? *That cat.* When Night Cat got himself up to the top of a tree and wouldn't come down? When the cat wanted to go out in the middle of the night? When he wanted food?

But standing at the bottom of the ladder, Night Cat in his arms, Sam remembered something else. *"If I get my hands on that cat!"* None of them had said it. It was just a wisp of a memory.

Sam stood there, petting the cat's back, and then the little spot under his chin. He leaned his head against Night Cat's. "I think we had a hard time," he whispered, even as he wondered why he'd said it. He went around to open the workroom door. With the cat inside, he hurried back along the side of the house.

He started up the ladder, the rungs bouncing under his feet. Night Cat was meowing again, pawing at the window-pane. As Sam looked down at the cat, his foot slipped.

He grabbed the next rung with both hands and held on, hoping no one could hear the cat. He didn't look down; he didn't look at anything except the wall of the house a few inches in front him.

He climbed that way until he reached the rung just below the top. With one hand he felt for the pipe that ran up next to him. It was cold under his fingers, swaying as he held it lightly.

He raised one foot, and then the other, to rest on the very top of the ladder. He crouched, then slowly stood up straight until he was directly in front of the window. Everything seemed to be moving, the pipe, the ladder, and a sudden wind that came from around the side of the house, but he pushed the window up with the palm of one hand and threw himself over the sill, hoping no one had heard.

Sam was tired now. He scooped up the small packet of papers that was lying next to the box, reached for the bundle of cloth, and put everything into the plastic bag. He saw the clipping on the floor and put it into the empty box. He didn't need it; he knew all about it now.

He was finished in the attic.

If only he didn't have to go down again. He took a breath, then backed out of the window, one hand on the pipe, the other holding the bag, feeling the ladder underneath him as it grated against the wall of the house. One foot hit the top rung, and then the other. The rest was easier. He let himself down, and at the bottom, leaned against the house until his heart stopped beating so loudly in his ears.

He dragged the ladder into the shed and went back upstairs, wondering about that bundle of fabric so familiar to him. He waited for the cat to pad into the bedroom, then closed the door and leaned against it to catch his breath.

He turned on the lamp next to his bed and put the pile of papers in his dresser. What he wanted was to look at that water-stained bundle. It was wrapped around something, with string tied in knots. It took time to work them out, and he untied them slowly, carefully, until the cloth fell open.

He sat there looking at the pieces inside, touching them, then took a chance. Closing the bedroom door behind him, he tiptoed down to the workroom for the tube of glue that was in the top drawer.

Upstairs again it was cold, and he threw the quilt around himself as he sat on the edge of the bed. He began to work on what he knew now was a sailboat, joining the pieces of wood, building the small cabin, gluing the tiny strands of rope that were guardrails.

When there were only two pieces of wood left, tall, thin, and rounded, he saw that the boat was meant to have a double mast. He dabbed glue into the small holes on the deck and fitted in the pieces, masts that were perfectly even, forming the number eleven.

Eleven.

Smoothing out the tiny sails as much as he could, he fixed them to the masts, and it was finished. He held it up, touching the sails gently, running his fingers over the wood, over the double mast.

It had been his boat.

He sat back. Mrs. Waring had pointed out the trees to him. What had she said? Something like *"You know by looking. They're trees, not anything else."*

His.

But it wasn't the way it looked, it was the feel of it. He would have known it if he'd been blind, known it with his fingers: his sailboat, not anything else. He thought about reading. If he'd been able to feel the letters with his fingers, cup his hands around the words, maybe it would have been different.

He'd sailed the boat when he was little. Kneeling at the edge of cool green water, he'd held a spool of string and watched the boat bob.

Was that true? Had it happened?

Yes. The string was gone, but the tiny nail for it was still there, rusty under his fingers.

He tried to think of what else he knew. He held the prow in his hands, willing himself to remember something about this boat with the double masts, to remember anything.

Where had he sailed it?

He squeezed his eyes shut, trying to think. Anima said, *"Your brain is a computer."* And Caroline had said, *"Everything that happens to you is up there."*

Something must be wrong with his brain. He couldn't dredge up one more thing.

But then he realized: the toy boat was a model of the one in the picture. Had the photo been taken from a different angle, he would have seen the tall matching masts. He might have remembered looking up at those masts against the blue sky.

What had happened to that boat? Someday, he promised himself, he'd build one like it.

He put the small boat carefully on the closet floor and turned off the lamp. He went to bed, the quilt around him, Night Cat at his feet.

As he fell asleep, he thought again of the boy with his flapping hands. And the woman shouting, "Give it to him,

Sam. Give it." The cat under the table, his back arched, hissing at her. *"If I get my hands on that cat!"*

His boat.

He'd wrapped his arms around it, but she'd reached for it, that huge woman with her shadow hovering over them on the wall. And he heard the sound of one of the masts snapping in two.

He lay there waiting for his heart to stop its fluttering, for the fear to lessen. Then he fumbled with the switch on the lamp and went to the closet, knowing what he'd see.

The mast on the right had been mended so carefully, you wouldn't know it had been broken unless you were looking for it.

He sank down onto the floor with the boat in his hands, mouth dry, so afraid. Suppose he belonged in that place with that woman? In that house with the kitchen white and cold?

Suppose he didn't belong here with Mack?

9
The Resource Room

Before school, Sam divided up the pack of papers he'd taken from the attic: half in one jacket pocket, half in the other. He brought them to school to show Caroline, but he wanted to check them out first, even though he'd be lucky to read two or three words himself.

After lunch, he went down to Mrs. Waring's Resource Room. It was a miserable place, with a spider wandering across the board and papers strewn over a table in back. Piles of books zigzagged halfway up the side of the wall: easy books with bent covers.

Mrs. Waring had told him once she thought the room was miserable too, even though there were a dozen plants on the windowsills and she'd pinned up pictures of the ocean with crashing waves.

Her desk was all right, though. One of the kids had brought in a glass bowl filled with sand and shells, and Mrs. Waring had added a striped wooden fish with an open mouth. The fish reminded Sam of Joseph, who sat across from him every day, scarfing down whatever he had left over from lunch.

Mrs. Waring passed out little books to practice context clues. It had sentences like *Carry your u_____ when it rains*. Joseph had written in *underwear*, trying to be funny, and even Mrs. Waring had laughed.

"Add sensible words," she said now.

Sam picked up his pen and bent his head over the booklet. At the same time, he slid one of the papers from the attic out of his pocket. He put it half inside the desk so he could look down at it. A bunch of numbers ran along the page in columns, with *a.m.* or *p.m.* on the sides. A schedule, then.

He took a quick look at Mrs. Waring to make sure she was still up front; she was watching him. He frowned as if he were trying to think of an answer. The question was idiot easy: *Tigers live in the j_____*. There was even a sketch of a tiger on one side. Not so easy to spell *jungle*, though.

At the top of the schedule were a couple of words: SUMMER—*something with an* F—HOURS. What?

Not *fair*. Not *free*. It had to make sense.

Mrs. Waring cleared her throat and he looked at his booklet. The next sentence needed a C, a country, China probably.

It reminded him of something that had happened in second grade. He looked over at the geraniums on the sill. They bloomed all winter, red and orange, with a sharp smell that came from their notched leaves and the damp soil. And only he and Mrs. Waring knew what was under the third pot.

That year, Mrs. Waring still came to his classroom door and waited until she caught his eye. Sometimes he wouldn't look at her, and one of the kids would yell, "Hey, that teacher is here."

"Where are you going?" Eric always asked.

"Going to China," he said once, angry.

"He can't spell *China*," Marcy had whispered. "He can't spell *cat*." Marcy, a pain even then.

"I want to spell *cat*," he'd told Mrs. Waring, and she'd curved the thumb of his left hand to meet his index finger, then pressed them both open a little. "If I leave my finger in the circle it becomes a G. See?"

"I don't care about G. I want to know *cat*."

"Yes, without the finger it's C. Use this hand, the one"—she pulled his left sleeve above his wrist, searching—"the one with the freckle. C for *cat*."

Someone called her from the office then, and she had to leave the Resource Room. He sat there waiting. His class passed on the way to recess, and he felt that heavy lump begin in his chest. He heard the tick of the clock overhead and put his head down. She still didn't come.

He stood up and went over to her desk. A small pair of

scissors was in a cup, its ends rounded, but they dug into the wood of the windowsill easily as he began to draw the C.

It was another teacher who found him, who saw him make the last bit of the curve in the C. And so he had to wait again, this time in the principal's office, while they called Mack.

"Sorry," he'd told Mack when he came in the door, looking worried. And "Sorry," he'd said to Mrs. Akins, the principal. He couldn't imagine what had made him carve up the wood of the sill. But the anger was still there, hot in his chest.

On the way home, Mack had said, "Pine, softwood. Easy to cut into and ruin." He'd put his hand on Sam's head.

"They left me," Sam said.

Mack had hesitated. "It's terrible to be alone."

"Something in my chest."

"Yes, I know."

He'd looked up at Mack. "Really?"

"The next time you're angry, wait until you get home. I'll show you how to get rid of that thing in your chest." Again that hesitation. "It's what I always did."

In the workroom, Mack had given him a block of wood with three large nails hammered a third of the way in. "Just hammer," Mack had said. "Hammer hard."

Sam had done it then, and dozens of times later. It always had something to do with not being able to read. He pounded in the nails until the block that was in his chest shrank away.

And the next day, Mrs. Waring had put her hand on his shoulder. *"We'll put a flowerpot over the C. And someday, we'll take the pot off and tell ourselves how hard this time was."*

Now he stared down at the booklet in front of him. Mack had said, *"It's terrible to be alone."*

Had Mack been alone too?

And *"It's what I always did."*

He'd never seen Mack angry. Never seen Mack pounding on a block of wood. But Mack had known how he felt.

"Let's go, guys," Mrs. Waring said from the front.

The third sentence in the booklet was something to do with water.

He looked down at the schedule. Ferry. That was it.

Summer Ferry Hours.

A boat schedule.

He wondered where the boat came from, and where it went.

10
Clues

From the corner of his eye, Sam saw movement in the door window. Caroline? Yes, there she was in the hall, her glasses sliding down her nose, one hand waving to get his attention.

Sam didn't look at Mrs. Waring. He went to the front of the room, picked up the pass, and was out of there. He went down the hall with Caroline, trying to think of a place to go.

They climbed to the third floor and stood at the top of the stairs. "One thing," Caroline said. "We should have remembered to look at the newspaper clipping to see where the accident happened."

"You're right," he said slowly, shaking his head.

"Even the name of the paper might help, and the date."

Sam blew air through his lips. The clipping was still in the attic. He'd have to go back again. But not on the ladder, not on the pipe. He'd be crazy to do that. He'd have to wait until he could go through Mack's bedroom.

Caroline was tapping his arm. "If we knew where the paper was from, we could use the computer in the Media Center and find the paper from the next day, and the day after that."

She leaned closer. "After all, we know you're alive." She grinned. "Barely."

He tried to grin back. "I have the other papers in my pocket. A ferry schedule. And one thing," he said, using her words. "I did a little figuring. The ferries ran often, so wherever it was, I don't think it was a long trip."

They sat on the top step, and he handed the rest of the papers to her.

"Here's a driver's license belonging to Mack," Caroline said. "It's from Florida." She pushed at her glasses, counting. "Eight years ago."

"I was three."

She looked up. "And here's something else."

He leaned over to see the scrap of paper, water-stained the way the sails of the boat had been: *Children's Home, 11th Street.*

He closed his eyes.

"Sam?"

He didn't answer. What he'd remembered had been true. The white kitchen, the terrible woman, the boy with the flapping hands, even Night Cat, darting under the table, afraid too.

The tile wall next to him was cold; he was cold. This was even worse than seeing that clipping for the first time. Mack

72

couldn't be his grandfather, Lydia couldn't be his grandmother. And who knew who his parents were?

There was a clanking sound on the railing: Mr. Ramon banging his keys. He glared at them from the bottom of the stairs. "Again I find you where you shouldn't be." He raised his eyebrows at Caroline. "Haven't you been here only a month or two?"

"I guess."

"And already you've linked up with Sam MacKenzie."

Bell.

Caroline's face was red as they took the stairs. They passed the assistant principal and scurried down the hall away from him.

Sam left her at the classroom door. "I'm sorry I got you in trouble," he said.

"I don't care. I'll be out of here in a couple of weeks, a month at most."

He went back to the Resource Room. Mrs. Waring glanced up at the wall clock when she saw him. "The time is up anyway."

"Sorry," he said again.

He couldn't stop thinking about it. Even when he got ready for bed, the words were in his head, in his throat: *Children's Home, 11th Street.*

"I wish you could talk," he told Night Cat. "And tell us where we've been."

And Caroline. He couldn't imagine school without her anymore.

Sam's Dream

The sails flapped overhead as they threaded their way
through the ice.
Islands of ice.
Someone at the tiller said, "They come from the sky."
Dropped by the Creator.
A house spun by, a flag.
He looked up and up, and saw—
an island, shaped like a heart.
In front was a rosy stone wall,
and higher,
a castle surrounded by trees, with more towers
than he could count. Roofs, tall and round, met the sky,
windows reflecting water.
Inside, men working.
Footsteps. Whose footsteps? His own?
He wanted to stay and look at that castle forever.
"A bold castle," someone said.
"Yes, bold."

11
The Castle

Middle Ages. Middle of the night. He'd been dreaming.

His eyes were closed, but he heard himself saying it aloud.

He sat up, and looked out the window. Yes, still dark, but he was wide awake. He swung his legs over the side of the bed, the floor cold underneath.

He fished around for his sneakers, his jeans, his warm sweatshirt, then went to the door with Night Cat behind him. He was losing the dream already. He stood there with his hand on the knob, willing himself to remember: a castle, but not like the pictures Mrs. Stanek had given him.

Downstairs, he stopped in the kitchen for a handful of Rice Krispies, then went to the workroom and flipped on the overhead light.

He looked at the picture he'd drawn for Caroline, and the castle they'd begun. They were wrong, something a little kid might draw. The castle would end up flat-sided, with only the turrets on top to give it any detail.

It wasn't like the dream castle at all. The dream castle didn't have turrets. It had towers, some rounded, some square, with roofs of tile, and the stone walls of the castle itself jutted out here and there—

Windows, too many to count.

High, so high above—

Above what?

That part of the dream was gone already. And even though he tried to bring it back, it was too late. People had been in the castle, people he knew, but they were gone too. Only the sound of loud feet, a kid's feet. His feet? Someone might have come after him, whispering, "Shhh."

But it was the dream castle he wanted to work on. It was the castle he'd build.

He could do this, really do it. Never mind school. Never mind Mrs. Stanek. Never mind anyone but himself. And Caroline. *Don't forget Caroline.*

He'd build this castle, finish it before she left, think about every detail.

He drew what he could remember on the back of his original drawing. Sketched it in, Mrs. Mallett, the art teacher, would have said. He didn't pay attention to scale, or to getting it exactly right. It was just so he'd remember before the dream lost itself entirely.

He thought of going back to bed, but he was wide awake. He reached for Anima's birthday book on the shelf over his table, paging through, searching, until he found a small cabinet with panels on the sides. He studied it; then in another few pages he found a drawing that showed a column. He saw how they were done; he could use both.

He took a second piece of paper and a ruler, counted, drew, erased, and started over, feeling the pull in his back from bending over for so long. But at last he had a drawing with scale to it.

He took wood from the bin and began to measure—
to draw in lines—
to cut the first piece—
and the second.

He kept going. Five pieces each for the sides, and he talked it out as he worked. "Two the same size for the ends, three smaller to form a section that juts out."

The front would need more, not only parts that jutted out into squares, but pieces to form columns.

It seemed like only minutes, but he realized it was much later when he looked up to see light coming in the window, the sky separating itself from the water. A pair of mourning doves cooed their song to each other, and a jay screeched from the top of a willow tree.

Sam worked on the wood until it was almost time for Mack to awaken; then he laid the pieces flat on his table.

Later he'd sand both sides of each one, even though only

one side would face out; the inside would be as smooth as the outside.

He covered all of it with a drop cloth. Mack knew that Sam and Caroline were working on a castle for school, but he'd never look at it until Sam asked him, invited him, to see it. Sam would show it only to Caroline until it was finished.

He went back upstairs and pulled off his sneakers, then opened the closet and took out the toy boat. He felt its smoothness, the curve of its body, and remembered sailing it, a vague picture of the green water, and wearing the sweater with a zipper.

He ran his hand over the two delicate masts with the almost invisible repair. This wasn't a boat someone had bought in a store. It was a boat that someone had made, taking pains with it, spending hours on it.

Mack.

It had to have been Mack.

Mack, who was afraid of water.

This was how Sam would build the castle, taking pains, spending hours. When he finished, it would last as long as this boat had. From Anima's book he'd learn how to cut the edges so they'd come together seamlessly. He'd learn how to cut glass. He'd learn everything he didn't know.

He couldn't wait to tell Caroline.

He slipped under the warm quilt, still holding the boat, and closed his eyes.

12
Onji

Late in the afternoon Mack was on his way to an auction, hoping to bring back a table to refinish. "It's a long ride and the weather is terrible," he told Sam, looking up at the leaden sky. "Stay and eat dinner with Onji."

Sam stood in the parking lot, shoulders hunched against the rain that had just begun, and watched him back the truck out. Mack would stop, lean out the window—

Yes. Halfway across the lot, Mack called back, "Be careful. Watch for customers until five. Lock—" He was gone, the tailpipe loud as he turned the corner and headed for the highway.

Sam stood there. Sometimes Mack was absentminded. He might be back looking for directions, his wallet, something. And suppose Mack found him upstairs on the way to the attic? It wasn't that the attic was off-limits. But what could he say he was doing up there? How could he explain?

After a few minutes, he went inside, shaking the rain off the way Night Cat would. He glanced up at the clock over Mack's worktable. He'd give it five minutes.

He began to smooth the edges of the castle walls he'd cut. He ran his hands over the pieces without looking at them, letting his fingers tell him where more of the plane was needed, or just a swipe with the sandpaper.

Outside, the wind had picked up, and it was getting dark. The windows rattled slightly. Good, let the customers stay home.

He looked up at the clock again; it seemed as if the hands weren't moving. He stared at it. Eventually it clicked another minute. Only Onji's van and Anima's blue Toyota were in the parking lot.

Now.

He went upstairs to Mack's room and stared at the armoire in the corner. He'd helped Mack build it; he'd stained the inside himself. He knew the shelf where he'd begun with the brush, the top where the stain had dripped into a narrow line. It was one of the first things he and Mack had done together.

So why couldn't he just open the armoire doors?

It was as if Mack's face were in front of him. The thick hair, the lines on his forehead. Mack's hand on his shoulder when Sam had finished a shelf. *"I couldn't have done better."*

How could he open the armoire and go through Mack's things? Bad enough to be up in the attic.

Mack's eyes. Blue eyes. Clear eyes.

Honest eyes.

Sam shook his head, trying to make sense of it all. Had Mack been honest with him? There were so many things Mack hadn't told him. He really knew only three things: a name, Bell, a place, the Children's Home, and the boat accident. Where did Mack fit?

He ran his hand over the armoire but couldn't make himself open the door.

He stood up on Mack's bed to reach for the rope with the loop and pull open the overhead door. He looked down to see the muddy imprint of his shoe. He should have realized. But never mind that yet.

He climbed the stairs, and in an instant had the clipping in his hand. He didn't bother to look at it, just folded it into his pocket, hearing the bells jangle on the outside door, and then the bellow, "Sam!"

Onji.

He slid down the stairs, almost flying, and reached for the loop to close the door, but he'd never be able to do it quietly enough. It always closed with such a bang. And Onji heard everything. He'd have to let it go.

"Sam?"

"Coming." He swept his hand over the muddy footprints on the bedcover, then went down the hall.

From the bottom of the stairs, Onji grinned at him. "What are you doing up there?"

"Nothing." He tried to look as if he'd really been doing nothing.

Onji pulled a handkerchief out of his pocket and wiped his face. "It's pouring out. Let's close up here and I'll fix us something to eat."

Sam looked back over his shoulder. "I'll be right over." *Go, Onji, please.*

"I'll check the back windows while you finish doing nothing," Onji said.

Sam listened to him go around the workroom, humming off-key under his breath. There was no help for it. Sam went down the stairs and met him at the door.

But suppose Mack came back before they finished eating? Came back to see the attic door gaping open over the bed? The quilt rumpled and muddy? How would Sam explain that to Mack?

He raised his hand. "Listen, Onji," then stopped. He followed Onji out, locking the door, and ran to the deli without a jacket.

Inside, the rain pounded on the windows; the panes were so steamy that everything outside was hidden. The door to Onji's office was open. Sam could see the computer and the photo of Onji's daughter, Ellie, on top.

Ellie was smiling and pointing to someone just out of the picture. Sam knew he was that someone, he'd heard it often enough. He'd just fallen into the water out back and was dripping wet, with reeds stuck to his legs.

"You're soaked, Sam." Onji wiped his hands on his huge apron and tossed him a towel. "We'll have trout, grilled, a twist of lemon, some slivers of almonds." He opened the massive refrigerator. "What could be better?"

"Can I help?" Sam tried to think of a reason to go back next door. "Did I lock the door? I'd better check."

Onji dumped a couple of carrots on the counter in front of him. "See if you can chop these up without cutting your fingers off. We'll eat them cold, crunchy. And don't worry, we locked the door."

The hands clicked off a minute on the clock on Onji's stove. Strange, when he wanted the time to go by in school, the clock hardly seemed to move. But now, time was flying, almost six o'clock.

Sam tried to figure when Mack would be back. Thirty minutes down to the outskirts of town at the most, say an hour or so at the auction, thirty minutes back. Thirty and an hour or two, plus another thirty—

"Are you listening?"

"What?"

Onji shook his head. "I was telling you how I caught this trout right under the bridge. It was cold in that river even with my hip boots and jacket. A skinny thing like you would have frozen to death."

"Hope you wore a cap." Sam looked at the rim of hair

around the edge of Onji's head, smiling, but still trying to add up the time. *Two hours.* Would it give him enough time to eat and to do something about the bedspread?

"Never mind about my cap." Onji pointed to the freezer with his thumb. "There's enough fish for both of us for weeks. We'll eat like kings every time Mack isn't around." He ran his hand over his head. "Imagine, Mack doesn't like to eat fish."

Easy to understand. Doesn't like the water, doesn't like fish. Sam took a breath. What could he say to Mack about being in the attic? *I know I don't belong here? I know I'm not your grandson?*

And then what?

He and Onji sat on stools at the high table in the middle of the deli kitchen, the fish on a platter in front of them, potatoes boiled and still steaming, and grilled tomatoes with breadcrumbs sprinkled across the top.

"Unique." Onji grinned at the carrots, cut into thick stumps. "A kid who can cut a piece of wood straight and true but can't manage a carrot."

"Knife's not sharp enough."

"Any sharper and you'd cut your hand off at the wrist." Onji slid a portion of fish onto Sam's plate, and the rest onto his own. "Good, right? The best. When we were kids your age, Mack and I, we'd fish outside the house even after dark trying to catch a walleye, or maybe one of those really big guys, muskellunge. What we did catch, Mack would give me." He pointed his fork at Sam. "Best friend I ever had. What would I do without him?"

Sam felt a lurch in his chest. But then he glanced up at the clock. Six more minutes gone.

"Five or six feet, those muskies." Onji leaned back on his stool. "Every summer there's a contest to see who can catch the biggest one. You'd have been too young to remember all that. Once on the boat, Mack came so close to catching a muskie. He was married by then. The fish yanked away the line, the reel, the rod."

Onji stopped to spear a piece of potato. "Mack was furious, jumping around. What a temper."

Sam looked up, really listening now.

"Other summers," Onji said, chewing, "Mack would be out before it was light, throwing stones up at my window. 'Go ahead,' I'd call down. By the time I was dressed he'd be out on the river in the boat. I'd just about see those white sails going under the bridge—"

Mack sailing? In the water? "Here? Was it here?"

Onji made a large curve with both hands. "A real bridge, huge, not like the one down the road at all."

Sam took a little of the tomato. "But Mack hates the water."

"Mack? Mack loved the water, swimming, sailing." Onji stopped suddenly, and bent his head toward his plate.

Sam kept eating; he made himself finish the last bite of fish before he asked, "So where did you fish, Onji, you and Mack?" *The place I was too young to remember.* Sam asked it easily, as if he were just talking, as if it weren't important. He pushed aside his plate.

Not easily enough. Onji had said more than he wanted.

Onji stood up, stretched, went to the refrigerator, and brought back a brick of ice cream. "Love this rocky road."

"Where did you say—" Sam didn't look at Onji; he stared at the empty fish platter.

"Try it." Onji slid a huge scoop of ice cream into a bowl for him. "I'll probably sell enough of this during the summer to make me rich."

He kept talking, never giving Sam a chance to ask. And then they heard the rattle of Mack's pickup truck as he pulled into the lot.

"Have to go," Sam said. He slid out from the table, hardly caring now what Onji might think. He slipped out the back door, across the muddy path.

Inside he yanked off his sneakers and tore up the stairs, banging the door shut up over the bed, wiping frantically at the mud, then darted into his bedroom.

The door opened downstairs, and Mack called up to him. "Sam, are you up there?"

"On my way down." Sam pulled the clipping out of his pocket, but there was no date, no place that might be written on top that he could see.

"Ready to go to Anima's?" Mack called.

"Sure, almost. Did you get any furniture?" Sam folded the paper carefully, slid it back into his pocket.

"Terrible pieces, not worth it."

"Sorry." Sam tried to catch his breath. "Listen, go on

over to Anima's. I'll be there in a few minutes. Homework," he said vaguely.

Another lie.

He listened as the outside door shut. He went to his room and found a piece of paper, a stubby pencil. He began to write: M. ENGRY. BIG FISH M. He drew the quick shape of a boat, a swimmer, Mack. What else had Onji said? BRIGE. On the bottom he wrote, I WAS THER. 2 ung.

He looked at the paper. He could read his own words even though no one else could.

He went downstairs to Anima's to listen to another Iroquois legend. "Masks," she read. "They were famous for their face masks, all with crooked noses. They were in honor of a giant who had a huge nose, and had frightened away the Spirit of Sickness, who'd come to prey on the people in the longhouse."

Mack was looking across the room at him, smiling a little.

Later that night Sam fell asleep, glad he hadn't opened the armoire. He'd never have been able to smile back at Mack. When he awoke it was early, five o'clock or so, and Night Cat didn't budge as he dressed and went down to the workroom.

He cut a piece for the base of the castle and began to work on the columns. By that time, he could smell bacon cooking at Onji's. Night Cat padded in, and overhead Mack stirred. It was time for breakfast.

Sam's Dream

A man with a scarf carried him over his shoulder.
Sam looked back at his house. His old house. Gone house.
"Don't leave the cat," he whispered.
"No," the man said.
Sam shivered.
"It's not far." The man wrapped his scarf around Sam. Black
scarf, bits of red in it.
Goodbye, old house.
Goodbye, river. Goodbye, big fish.
Up ahead, that terrible house.
Eleven.

13
Knights

"Let me tell you—" Sam began as the class line snaked its way to the music room.

"No, let me tell you," Caroline whispered back, a smudge of lipstick on her braces. "Call your grandfather and tell him you're coming to my house after school today." Before he could answer she held up her hand. "Don't ask. You'll see."

"All right." There wasn't time for more, anyway.

When the dismissal bell rang he hurried down the hall. He hoped Caroline wouldn't know he was embarrassed about going to her house. *"Hanging out with girls?"* Eric would joke.

Caroline knew, though, and hung back until they

reached the corner. "That Eric." She nudged Sam. "All right, your turn to talk."

He gave her the clipping, and she leaned against a tree, staring at it. "No date, no name. Too bad."

He took the clipping back. It would have been so easy, too easy. "I have the other papers for later." He touched his pocket, then handed her his own paper. "I took notes."

"Whooo. Who could read—"

"I can."

"I'll tape it in the book, then." Her eyebrows were raised over her glasses. "But you'd better translate."

He began with Onji telling him about Mack's temper, though Sam had never seen Mack angry once. He told her about the boat, and swimming, though he knew Mack was afraid of the water. He told her about huge fish, fish that he was too young to remember. "I was there, Caroline, where they grew up."

And something else. "I dreamed—" He broke off. "I think it was all nearby, all together: a river, the house where I'd lived with my mother, another place—" It was vague in his mind. "All near where Mack and Onji grew up."

By the time he finished, they were walking up the path to the boxy blue house where Caroline and her family were staying. Sam glanced at the windows: no curtains, but her mother was standing there, Caroline's little sister next to her, both of them waving.

"My father's painting on the river somewhere," Caroline said.

Her mother opened the door. Her sneakers were untied, her hair down almost to her waist. It was about the same color as Caroline's but it looked as if she hadn't combed it in a week.

It was easy to see why. She was running a pencil through her hair with one hand, pushing tangled strands off her face with the other, making the whole thing worse. And what was that stuff under her fingernails? Had Caroline said something about clay?

Her mother led the way into a tiny kitchen, bending down to open cabinets, and then the refrigerator. "I was supposed to get something for you to eat—"

"That's all right."

"No, I did get something. It's just a question of where I put it." She smiled at Sam over her shoulder. "Ah, here, strawberries." She looked a little uneasy. "You do like strawberries, right?"

"Sure."

She pulled a pot out of the closet underneath the counter, and a couple of chocolate bars from a drawer. "We'll melt these, and dip—"

She was like Caroline, just like Caroline. "Chocolate-covered strawberries," he said. "Cool."

"And we have cookies, so we can dip them, too." She swept a pile of books and papers off the table onto a chair.

They sat at the table, chocolate dripping on the white top. Little Denise ran her finger across it, licking off the drips.

Caroline looked happy with all this. "Just wait, Sam."

And all this time, her mother stared at him. "You're right," she told Caroline. "I can do this. He has an easy face." She turned to Sam. "Don't take forever with that. Eat fast, we have things to do."

They went into what was probably supposed to be a bedroom, but instead was the mother's workroom. It was a gigantic mess.

Sam loved it.

"I didn't have time to set up my kiln," she said. "I guess Caroline told you we'll be leaving soon."

He didn't want to think about that. Instead he looked at the things taped to the walls: paint swatches, a shamrock, an old paper fan, and on a table, jars filled with brushes and sharp little knives. In the center was a mound of clay.

"Sit there, right in front of me." Caroline's mother pointed.

She pulled a chair up in front of him and closed her eyes. "Excuse me." She ran her fingers, a little sticky, over his face, his nose, his chin.

He didn't move; he knew his face was red.

She opened her eyes, sat back. "A snap." She reached behind her for bits of clay, and began to shape the clay into a figure.

"She's going to make knights for the castle," Caroline said, "with your face. She'll make one or two with those things over their heads—"

"Helmets?"

"Yes. So you won't see that it's you, but the rest—"

Caroline's mother held up the figure and tilted her head. "Almost." She smoothed the head and shoulders. "Would it be too nerdy," she asked, "to have one lady? And young knights?"

"Squires," he said. "Why not?"

Moments later, she set the finished figure on the table. "A bold knight," she said.

Caroline peered over Sam's shoulder. "You have to look closely to see that it's you, but it really is, isn't it? Even the little scar above the eyebrow."

He raised his hand to his face and ran his fingers over his forehead, his nose, as she had done. She had captured him exactly. "How did you do that?" He stopped. He thought of something else. "What did you say?"

"A bold knight," she said.

Had he dreamed that? A bold knight? A bold castle?

But he had no time to think about it. Caroline was dragging him into their family room. There was a television at one end, a couch, a table, and a couple of chairs at the other. Boxes were piled against the wall.

Caroline waved her hand at them. "We never unpacked, only the things we absolutely needed."

They sat on the couch with the small table in front of it. "Let's see what you have," Caroline said.

He pulled the papers out of his pocket, messy now,

the rubber bands broken. They went through the driver's license, the ferry schedule, the scrap of paper: *Children's Home, 11th Street*.

Next was a picture of Mack. He stood stiffly next to a woman, probably Lydia. They were leaning against the glass window of a hardware store, Clayton's. Last was a picture of a young girl sitting against a tree with water in the background. He'd seen that one before. *"Julia, your mother,"* Mack had said.

Sam wondered who she really was.

And that was all.

14
Anima's Restaurant

On Tuesday morning Sam was awake early again. Downstairs, he cut little pieces of glass and began to fit them into the small spaces he'd cut into the castle walls. He hurried now, anxious to join the walls together.

The tiny windows were longer than they were wide, almost slits. He ran glue along the edges, his hands sticky with it, the rectangles so small it took forever to put in each one. He just finished before it was time to get ready for school.

That afternoon, Mack had varnished the cabinet he'd made for Anima, and the four of them stood there in the empty restaurant, looking at it. "The best you've ever done, Mack," Anima said.

Mack ran his hand along the wood, testing its smooth-ness. He and Mack did that with everything, always feeling for the last rough spots. Mack glanced over at him, and his eyes crinkled the way they did when he was about to smile. Sam smiled back and nodded. They were thinking the same thing. The wood would be smooth as glass.

Onji clapped his hand on Mack's shoulder. "Perfect, like everything you've ever done."

Mack shook his head, a movement so quick Sam would have missed it ordinarily. If only he knew what Mack was thinking.

But then Anima said, "We'll have a celebration, all of us. And isn't your friend Caroline coming tomorrow? Ask her to stay for dinner." She was laughing. "She hasn't lived until she's tasted my chicken curry."

"As long as she doesn't know the ingredients."

Anima had an innocent look on her face. "Everyone likes chicken." Her delicate hands waved. "Onions and lemons—"

"It's the coriander, the cumin."

"Good. I'll make an Indian cook out of you one of these days."

The next afternoon, Caroline came, and they went into the workroom. She'd brought a box of carefully wrapped knights with her. She opened the one on top.

"The medieval lady." He held it up. "She looks just like you."

They perched on chairs in front of the table, and she

held the wall pieces as he glued them together and set them on the base. They stood back. "It's a castle," she said. "It's really a castle. We should name it."

He was surprised; he'd thought they'd talked about it. "Bold," he said. "Bold Castle."

"Just right," she said, nodding.

"It fits, doesn't it?" He leaned over to show her where the surrounding wall would be, and she pulled a mirror out of her bag. "Guess I can do without this. You can use it for a moat."

Why not? "Neat."

Caroline wrote it all down, but then she glanced up, twisting her bracelets anxiously. "We have to hurry."

"We have plenty of time. Anima said six o'clock. Onji's going to close early—"

"I don't mean that. My father's going to meet someone tonight about teaching art in a college. Can you imagine? He says he wants to settle down. My mother said it would be permanent; she was dancing around the kitchen." She raised her hand. "Not here. It won't be here."

Caroline stopped and went on in a voice so low he could hardly hear her. "One more school. I'll have to stand at the classroom door and all the faces will be strange, staring at me—"

She ran her hand over the castle wall. "But this is going to be the most perfect thing, Sam. If only I could live inside, hidden away with my family forever."

"I'll build you a room and put the medieval lady inside.

No one will know you're in there, but you'll be there forever."

He saw a quick flash of tears in her eyes. "And you can remember it when you go away." He tried to think of something else to say, something easy, something that would take them away from her leaving. "Just a few rough spots here and there. Look." He picked up the sandpaper and handed it to her. "If you rub lightly—"

She began to work with the sandpaper, her head tilted, her hair covering the side of her face. She brushed it back impatiently and looked out at the parking lot. "There's gravel out there. Maybe we could put a little of that around the edge and make a path."

He nodded. Did they have gravel in the days of castles? They might have had crushed stone. And if not, it was their castle, after all.

And then it was time to go to Anima's. They walked around in front of the building with Mack, circling Night Cat, who was washing one paw. A sign on the door said CLOSED TONIGHT FOR A PRIVATE PARTY.

"That's us," Sam said.

Inside the restaurant, one table had been set up in the middle of the room for all of them. Even Onji's daughter, Ellie, was there.

Anima, her face red from the heat of the oven, brought out one tray after another, nodding at Caroline. "I love the cabinet Mack made for me, and someday Sam will be able to do the same thing."

Sam looked toward the side of the room. Mack had used pine; he'd carved figures of birds into it, the birds they saw out back. He'd used antique brass for the handles and hinges.

Sam thought about what Anima had said. He couldn't do something like this cabinet yet, but someday he would. Mack's words: *"You have a gift."*

Could you have only one gift? He needed more. He needed Caroline to stay; he needed to know more about himself, Sam Bell. And suppose he could read? Thinking about having all of it was almost like telling himself the fairy tales Anima read, with genies and godmothers granting wishes.

Onji spread his hands wide. "Pretty sad when my greatest accomplishment is a hot pastrami sandwich."

Sam looked across the table at Caroline. She was grinning at him. She remembered the first day in the cafeteria with the pastrami sandwich and the Gummi Bears. "Your sandwiches are the best," she told Onji. "Sam is so lucky."

Anima sat, and they began to eat, crunchy vegetables in a thick, spicy coating. "Will you stay and listen to me read tonight?" Anima asked Caroline.

"Of course," Mack said. "Sam and I will drive her home afterward."

"Good," Anima said, going to the kitchen for more food.

"I'll stay too," Ellie said. "A great dinner, then reading afterward. Anima's stories." She tapped Onji's shoulder. "Remember that one about the old Iroquois legend? The islands the Creator dropped in the river, thousands of them?

Wasn't it where you and Mack grew up, where all of us were born?"

Mack said, "I'll go help Anima," and Ellie said, "I will too," and by the time they came back with almond pudding in small flowered bowls, the story was forgotten.

Except that it was all Sam thought about for the rest of the meal. ". . . *where all of us were born.*" It was the place he wanted to know about.

15
The Media Center

It rained the next morning, with thunder rolling across the sky, and even though Sam and Eric ran from the bus across the schoolyard, their shirts were soaked.

Sam went into the classroom, stamping the water out of his sneakers. Caroline was standing at her desk, squeezing the ends of her hair, drops of water spraying the desk in front of her.

A sub was there today. Caroline motioned to Sam and whispered, "Let's go down to the Media Center."

They slipped out and went down the hall. "Great to have a sub," Sam said. "She'll never miss us." He jumped up to touch the ceiling light. "Ellie was talking last night—" he began.

"Yes. She said something about thousands of islands. Maybe ten thousand."

They pushed open the doors. A kindergarten class was having a story hour, and Mrs. Hurd, the librarian, glanced up absently. "You might have dried yourselves off."

"Just using the computer," Caroline said. "We'll be careful."

They sat next to each other, Caroline's notebook between them. "You know how to use the computer?" she asked.

"Anyone can press a button." He grinned at her, but he was shivering. Maybe it was because his shirt was still wet, sticking to him, or maybe it was because of what might be there on the computer.

Caroline tapped his arm. "Punch in 'ten thousand islands.' "

Easy to punch in 10,000. He hesitated, but how to spell *islands?*

She didn't wait; she leaned over to type it in for him, and instantly, a page of blue came up with numbers that stood out and were repeated over and over among the words.

"Florida," she said.

He whispered it, closing his eyes. *Florida?*

Mack's driver's license.

Caroline began to read. "Everglades, vacation paradise, boating. There are pictures here too, Sam." She pointed with the mouse to bring the pictures up: mossy green trees reflected in swampy water, fishing boats under blue skies, and sails on the horizon.

Could he remember any of that? Could he picture

sailing that little toy boat there, holding the string as it bobbed along on the edge of the water? "Big fish," he said. "Game fish, I think you call them. Do you see anything—"

She scrolled down and clicked. Immediately there was a photo of a huge fish coming up out of the water, glinting silver, its tail a fan. The fisherman, back arched, at the stern of a sailboat—it even had a double mast—strained to bring in the fish.

Florida.

The kindergarten class moved out of the Media Center and Mrs. Hurd wandered over to them. "What are you working on?"

Caroline's face flushed. "We have a project on the Middle Ages in Mrs. Stanek's room. We have to build a castle, knights . . ." Her voice trailed off. Her fingers were crossed.

Mrs. Hurd squinted at the screen. "I don't think Florida had anything to do with the Middle Ages. I'm not sure the Europeans had even gotten to the Everglades yet."

"We just—" Sam said.

"I think you'd better go back to your classroom. And find some towels, dry yourselves off."

They went out and stopped at the fountain for water. "Wet inside and out," Caroline said.

"It's not right."

"What? Walking out of the classroom without permission? Getting the library floor wet? Mrs. Hurd sending us back? What, Sam-I-Am?"

He ran his hands over his arms. He was still cold. "Florida doesn't feel right."

She wiped her mouth. "But Mack's license—"

"I dream of cold. The water is gray, not blue; it's almost black."

She nodded uncertainly.

He raised one shoulder. "Dreams aren't always right, I guess, but still—"

She sighed. "So maybe the legend doesn't fit."

The door of their classroom opened and the kids barreled out, the sub in back of them.

"Art," Caroline said. "I forgot."

"Do you two belong to this class?" the sub said as they fell into line.

"They were probably in the Media Center," Marcy said.

"Thank you, Marcy," the sub said.

"Yes, thank you," Sam echoed under his breath.

By that time they were filing into the art room. The teacher gave out paper. Free drawing.

Sam began to sketch. A sailboat with a double mast that looked like eleven. Water that was gray, the boat almost over on its side. Was he drawing the boat in the photo from the attic? Was it the toy boat? Or maybe it was a boat he'd like to build someday.

Which one?

He couldn't be sure.

16
Onji's Office

In the workroom that afternoon, Sam cleared the table to make room. Caroline had left her notebook. He flipped it open to the front. *Castle by Sam and Caroline*. Easy to read, and some of the other words weren't so hard either. They were written down in rows: *Plywood, e-z cut, tall, mist*, another word that had to be *moat*, one that might have been *gravel. Sandpaper*.

In the back of the notebook were more words: some of hers, and the page he'd written. *Big fish M*.

He put the notebook aside and opened Anima's book to a drawing. He began to cut the tower roofs, shaping them like pizzas, each circle cut into six pieces. The center points would be the peaks, and they'd fan out over the towers.

He leaned over the castle without its roof. He'd added a

room just for Caroline, and once the roofs were put on top, no one would be able to see inside. It would be just for her.

Perfect, he could almost hear her say.

He looked out the half-opened window at the back of the workroom. The leaves that covered the trees were still pale and new looking, but shoots of wild onion poked up in patches among the reeds at the water's edge. It was really spring.

Caroline's voice was in his head: *Hurry, hurry.*

Beyond the reeds, Mack sat on Anima's bench, head up to catch the sun. Onji stood in the water in old hip boots and his waterproof jacket, fishing. Ellie must be there today to take care of the deli.

Mack and Onji were laughing. "Your feet are so big you're mucking up the whole bottom," Mack was saying. "The fish need glasses to see the bait."

What was the name of that fish Onji had talked about? M. Sam hummed the sound, smoothing most of the small roof pieces before he remembered. *Muskie.*

Sam threw the cloth over the castle and went around back to go to the deli. Mack and Onji saw him and raised their hands.

"Catch a pickerel for dinner, Onji," Sam called.

"Maybe. I'll try."

In the deli kitchen Ellie was stirring a pot of onion soup on the huge stove. "Want a taste?"

"I'll wait. I just want to use the computer in Onji's office. All right?"

"Why not?" Ellie said. "Dad would say, 'Goodbye, computer, when Sam gets his hands on it.'"

"I'm sure-handed." Sam went into the small office. He pressed the On button and moved the cursor to get to the Internet.

Muskie.

He whispered it, trying to sound it out. "Muskie."

"Are you talking to yourself back there?" Ellie called.

"Listen and learn," Sam called back. One of Mrs. Stanek's favorite things to say.

But Ellie was singing, something about ants going up a hill, while she rattled around in drawers.

Sam tried the word with an *a*, *maskie*, then an *e*, *meskie*, and an *o*, *moskie*.

It was when he spelled it with a *u* that the printing came up, filling the screen. Small print, line after line of it, shape after shape. He felt the impossibility of it, anger bursting in his chest. It was right there in front of him, but he couldn't read it. Some of it, of course, *cold water*, *game fish*, but as for the rest—

If only he could read.

He must have said something aloud, made some kind of sound, because he heard Ellie say, "Sam?" and her heavy footsteps came around the kitchen table toward the computer room.

Sam reached out to hit the Escape button but missed, hitting one of the letter keys, and then she was looking over his shoulder and pointing. "Ah, it's the Thousand Islands."

He sat entirely still.

Her fingers went to the screen, to the map in the right-hand corner. "Here's where Dad and Mack grew up, and me, too. Where the Iroquois lived. The St. Lawrence River."

His throat was too thick for him to say anything.

"Remember the legend of the masks?"

"All of them different, but with crooked noses—" He swallowed, found his voice: "—to honor the giant who chased the Spirit of Sickness away."

"And the other one, of course."

"The Thousand Islands," he said.

"Yup," Ellie said. "Right there in the St. Lawrence River."

There between his own state, New York, and Canada.

He pressed the Escape button, and all of it disappeared.

"How about a sandwich?" Ellie asked. "A hero, maybe, or some chicken parm? Some of the soup?"

He shook his head. "No, thanks, I have to get back." He turned and gave her a hug.

"What's that for?" she asked, smiling.

"That's for nothing." He went back to the woodworking room and saw Caroline's green notebook on top of his table.

He flipped it open to the back, seeing the list Caroline had written, and the paper with his words: *I WAS THER*.

It needed an *e, there*. Yes. He'd been there. He added *1000 ilands* . . . something wrong with that, but never mind. And *St. L*.

He closed his eyes. He saw Mack sailing under a bridge

that he felt sure must be there, white sails, a double mast. He pictured the huge fish underneath like gray shadows, the muskies.

And not far from there must be the place where the woman had given his boat away, the place that terrified him, the Children's Home.

Sam's Dream

People yelling. Angry. Screaming.
The woman.
A man.
Doors banging.
His door was next.

17
Leaving

It was so hot that Mrs. Stanek threw up her hands after collecting lunch money. "Let's go outside and have an extra recess, before I melt away."

Eric ran to the closet for the bag of soccer balls, and the rest of them lined up, almost falling over each other.

It was the chance Sam had been waiting for. Telling Caroline what he'd found out was almost as good as knowing it himself.

He watched while a soccer game started and kids began to choose up sides for a baseball game. "Come on, MacKenzie," Eric yelled. "We need you at third base."

"Too hot," he called back. "Sorry." He went to look for Caroline.

She was leaning up against the Cyclone fence, her finger in her book to mark her place.

"The Thousand Islands," he said. "Not ten thousand. They're in the St. Lawrence River." The words tumbled out as if he couldn't say them fast enough. "I should have known."

She was turned away from him, staring out at the street. "I'm glad you found that much." Her voice sounded odd.

He moved around to see her face. She wasn't crying, but she had been. Her eyes were swollen, the lids pink, and her golden eyelashes were clumped together, darker than usual.

"You left the notebook in the workroom," he said, holding it out.

She reached for it absently and put it in her pocket.

"We're almost ready to put the roofs on the castle." He was hardly thinking of what he was saying. "I just want to paint the room I made for you." He stopped and began again. "We can do some of it this afternoon."

She took her finger out of her book; it closed with a tiny snap. "Go away, Sam-I-Am. Please."

Had he heard her right? He reached back, poking his fingers into the fence's chain links. "What is it? What's the matter?" he asked, even though he was sure he knew.

"I told you I had no time for friends." Her eyes welled up with tears, and she turned away from the yard to face the fence again. Her voice was muffled. "Why did you want me to be your friend?"

He didn't know what to say. How could he say it was because he wanted her to read the papers in the box? How could he say it was the castle? How could he say it had just happened? And that afterward, being her friend was as important as everything else? More important. "You're leaving, aren't you?"

She sounded breathless. "Sunday."

"But tomorrow's Saturday." He stopped. "We haven't finished the castle."

"And we don't know all about you. Listen, my mother pulled the suitcases out last night. Most of the boxes were never unpacked."

The kids were yelling as they played ball, and Mrs. Stanek stood in front of the brick wall of the school, her eyes closed. He wished he could yell at everyone to stop, yell at them to do something.

He kept shaking his head as Caroline spoke. "We'll roll up the sheets and the blankets, put everything from the medicine cabinet in a plastic bag." Her bracelets jangled against each other. "We've done all this before. But my father promised it's the last time. He's going to teach sunsets instead of drawing them. He promised."

She brushed at her face. "On Monday, I'll be in a new school, the third this year."

"But the castle." *Bringing it to school. The two of them putting it on the table in the back of the room. What Mrs. Stanek might have said, what the kids would have said. The new kid and the kid who could hardly read had done this. The best project in the room, the first time for him.*

A ball bounced across the yard toward them, and he

picked it up and tossed it back. "Come with me first this afternoon. We'll finish the castle. You'll take it with you."

Who cared about what the class thought? She could have the castle, keep it in her room, she'd remember—

"Oh, Sam, I have to help my mother." She walked away from him, keeping close to the fence, her back straight. She was crying again.

He wanted to go after her, or call after her, but he didn't know what to say. Mack had told him once, *"Onji always knows what to say, but it's hard for me."*

Mrs. Stanek blew her whistle; it was time to go in.

"You're going to miss the medieval feast," he called after Caroline, trying to make her smile.

"Pease porridge hot," she said over her shoulder. Marcy Albert said that twenty times a day.

They were the last ones in the schoolyard. Mr. Ramon was coming across the yard and waved at them to hurry.

They followed the rest of the class up the stairs and into the classroom. "I have something for you," Caroline said. "I made it myself. Not so great, but anyway—you'll see when you get home."

The day went by in a blur. They sat together at lunch, and when it was time for him to go to Mrs. Waring's room, he whispered, "Don't leave before I come back."

But she was gone by the time Mrs. Waring finally let them go; the room was empty, except for the small package on his desk.

One day left.

18
The Phone Call

In the workroom, Sam unwrapped the package. It was a horse, with one leg a little shorter than the others, the face goofy. He held it up; it was just the kind of thing Caroline would make. He patted its clay back and leaned it against the plane so it would stay upright.

He took the cloth off the castle. It still needed the roofs for the towers; the pie-shaped pieces were spread out next to it.

He looked inside at the room he'd made for Caroline. Why should he finish it now? But how could he not?

Mack had sample cans of paint on a shelf under the window near the front door. Some of them were metallic: gold and silver, and a tangerine color almost like Caroline's hair. He opened that one and painted the room with a small brush, bending over, angling his head to see into the corners. *"The brush you use is so important,"* Mack always said, *"the size, the shape."* Sam tried to concentrate on that, the brush, the strokes, the look of the hidden room, instead of Caroline's leaving.

The bell jangled over the door behind him, and a woman came in holding a small oval table in her arms.

Sam might have called Mack to come down. He was just upstairs in the kitchen having a cup of tea. He'd been here working all day while Sam was in school. "Tired feet," he'd said as he went up the stairs. "Bone tired."

Instead Sam took the table from the woman. She showed him a cut on the top. "The dog chased the cat through the living room, the lamp went over. I was so furious—"

"Pine," Sam said. "Soft wood. Easy to cut into. Too easy."

"But the dog's more important than the table, after all. Can you fix it?"

He ran his thumb over it. Deep. It would take layers of filler, days of sanding, staining. "We can do it."

The phone rang.

"Just a second." He went to the window table and picked it up. "Mack's Woodworking."

"Sam?"

It was Caroline. He felt himself smile. "Yes."

"Listen."

The woman with the table cleared her throat.

"There's something we have to do tomorrow."

"I'm in a bit of a hurry," the woman said. "Who knows what the dog is doing now?"

"Can you hold on?" he asked Caroline. "Just for a second?" He put the phone down and gave Mack's work pad to the woman. "Just your name and a phone number."

"I don't have my glasses." The woman pushed the pad back at him.

There was always something to remind him about the reading. But Mack had taught him to ask customers to spell their names. And if there was something special that needed to be done, something that wasn't obvious, he just had to remember.

"Your name?" He tried not to sound impatient.

"Marie Judson," the woman said absently as she went around him and walked toward the castle. She reached out.

He didn't want her to touch it. "The paint is wet." He could spell *Judson*, two pieces to it. He didn't have to bother with the first name, but hurry, he told himself, Caroline was waiting.

"That's a beautiful model," the woman said. "I've seen a castle like that."

He looked back at the phone.

"Is it the one on Heart Island?"

He spread out his hands. "It's just—" He shook his head. "We'll call you as soon as the table's ready."

She smiled. "Hope you don't have a dog."

"A cat," he said, holding the phone again.

"My mother gave me the table years ago. It was in her living room."

He motioned with the phone. "I have to get this. Sometimes people won't wait."

"No patience," she said, and went out the door.

He put the phone to his ear. "Caroline?"

"Tomorrow's Saturday, and we can have the whole day together. My mother said she doesn't need me, that I can come over to the workshop."

He looked toward the castle. All day tomorrow.

"We can't do that, though." She was whispering, her voice rushed.

He shook his head. "Wait a minute."

"I've looked up the bus schedule. I have babysitting money."

"Whoa."

"I've found the Children's Home, Eleventh Street. I'll meet you at the bus stop in town. Nine o'clock."

The phone clicked and she was gone. He ran his fingers over the woman's table, his mouth dry.

Was he really going back to that house tomorrow, back to the woman, and maybe to the boy with the flapping hands?

And then another thought. What was he going to tell Mack?

19
The Children's Home

Sam was awake half the night. Did he really want to do this?

He stumbled out of bed in the morning, and dressed. Mack was in the workroom. Sam took a breath. "I'm going to see Caroline. It's her last day."

Mack nodded. "Nice. Go ahead. It's warm, sunny. A good idea."

If Mack knew, really knew, Sam thought. He ate a quick breakfast of juice and muffins at Onji's, and asked for an extra sandwich for Caroline. "Her last day," he said again.

Onji looked up, a roll in his hand. "A picnic. Good."

Five minutes later, Sam was jogging along the road. Breathless, he reached the stores at the edge of town. Caroline was just ahead of him, wearing a purple hat, and a wooden necklace over her sweater. She grabbed his hand and tugged as she started to run. "We're late," she said.

He'd never held hands with a girl before. Her hands were warm, and a little smaller than his. It made him smile even though he couldn't imagine how this day would end.

"We may have missed the bus," she said. "We'll have to wait a half hour for the next one."

They crossed the street in front of the bank, and went to stand at the stop in front of the Circle Diner. The bus was nowhere in sight. "I'll ask inside," he said as Caroline bent to close the Velcro on her sneakers.

He poked his head in the door. "Did the bus leave yet?"

Tom at the counter hardly looked at him. "New York City or west?"

"West," Caroline called in.

"Just missed it."

Caroline rolled her eyes. "Let's go sit in a booth. I have plenty of money."

He had money too, but he couldn't imagine swallowing anything. He followed her inside the empty diner and slid into the booth on the end.

They sat there, not talking, until Tom brought the hot chocolates Caroline had called for across the room.

Sam ignored his cup with the small marshmallows floating on top. "Tell me what's going on." He leaned across the table.

She pulled out the notebook. "While you were doing nothing—"

He grinned.

"I looked at the map. I started at the towns along the St. Lawrence River and looked on the Internet, trying to link two things together with the phone information. The Children's Home and Clayton's. You know, the picture—"

"Of Mack and Lydia in front of the hardware store."

"There's a town called Clayton."

He took a breath.

"But that's not it. There's another town called Waterway." She frowned. "Waterway? And there's a Clayton's hardware store, and—"

"The Children's Home."

"Well, almost. There's an Eleventh Street."

He sat back. They wouldn't find anything. He wanted to laugh with surprise and a feeling that was something like relief. Maybe he didn't have to know about himself. Maybe he could just stay with Mack, and Anima, and Onji forever.

Onji always talked about wild-goose chases. And this would be a neat wild-goose chase. They'd take the bus, and eat Onji's lunch. It was a great day, after all; the sun was shining. They'd have a last day they'd always remember. He picked up the mug of chocolate and downed it in one gulp.

She must have been thinking the same thing. She stretched. "Just think, we'll have this whole scoop of a day." She hesitated. "One thing." She leaned closer, her eyes so large, those freckles like constellations.

One thing. Her favorite thing to say.

"I might be wrong. And if I am, let's write this all out for you before I go." She opened her notebook. "Begin at the beginning."

The chocolate was suddenly a lump in his stomach, the marshmallows so gluey, he could still taste them on his tongue.

Caroline was holding a pen. "Okay. Go," she said.

The beginning. "My parents died."

The book was between them; she wrote at an angle. *Parents*. He could see that.

"I ended up in the Children's Home."

"In the same town?"

In Mack's town, Onji's town. "Yes, I think so."

Her head was bent, and he didn't bother to read what she wrote now.

"A terrible woman, a boy who took my boat. She slapped—Mean to all of us, I think. To the cat. I was so afraid for the cat." Something tugged at the edge of his mind. Mack had built the toy boat for him, he was sure of it. He must have known Mack while he was at the home. How did that fit? He thought of footsteps in a castle. The sound of a hammer. Banging doors.

There was no time to tell Caroline more. The bus was pulling up in front of the diner. He left money on the table, and they boarded the bus, stopping to pay, in back of an old man carrying a fishing rod.

In one of the backseats, Caroline opened her lunch, a mess of a sandwich, two slabs of cheese surrounded by bread. "Horrible," he said. "How can you still be hungry?"

"I'm always hungry."

"Good. I have lunch for you."

They sat there, not talking. He watched the hills flatten out. The bus traveled along next to a fast-moving stream, and people fished from rocks along the way.

After a while Sam was hungry too, but not hungry enough for the meatball hero. He dug into the bag to find two packages of saltines. He handed one to Caroline, then leaned against the window, chewing.

Every once in a while, the bus stopped to pick up passengers or to let them off. The man with the fishing rod nodded to them as he got off at the back door.

And then the driver called out, "Waterway, New York," and they went down the steps. Nothing looked familiar to Sam: not the stores on the main street, not the park with its benches at one end, not the wooden church with its square steeple at the other.

Caroline glanced at him. "I'm going into the bakery. I'll ask."

"Don't. Suppose—" Was this the place? And if it was, he almost felt that store owners would see him: *There's that kid from the home, the kid from the boating accident.*

"Sam, it was years ago. Do you think you still look like the kid in the picture? Do you think anyone would know who you are?"

Before he could answer, she disappeared inside the store. He leaned against the brick wall, sun-warmed even this early in the day.

She was back. "There is a children's home, was a children's home. The baker told me how to get there. Amazing, isn't it?"

Sam felt the sudden heat in his face. He swallowed against the catch in his throat.

Caroline took his hand again, and they went down the street past the church and turned onto a small road that wound its way along in back of the main part of the town.

He walked more slowly, and then at the second turn, where trees began to meet over the path, he stopped. "Wait a minute," he said. "Just wait—"

"It's there, but it isn't. It was closed down years ago." Caroline tugged at his hand. "No one's there, Sam."

He walked with her up a lane that was choked with dandelions showing their yellow tops. Gravel, gray and scattered, crunched under their feet. He remembered the sound of that gravel. "Someone brought me here, carried me on his shoulder. I was crying, cold, and he put his scarf around me."

"I'm sorry, Sam." Her voice was low. "I'm so sorry for that little kid."

He saw the scarf clearly, dark with flecks of red, felt the warmth of it against his cheek, but he couldn't see the man's face.

"Was it Mack?" Caroline asked.

"No, not Mack. I don't think it was anyone I knew." He pieced it out in his mind. *Steps.* No one to take him, probably no family, and someone, a neighbor maybe, had brought him here. He remembered carrying the small sailboat.

Sam took a step, turned a corner. The building appeared suddenly in front of him. He stepped back, almost as if he'd been hit. It was really there, that terrible place, much more than a house, with its massive double doors in front, the number eleven over them, smaller doors on each end. Eleven, of course.

He leaned against a tree, almost forgetting that Caroline was watching him. He heard the sound of banging doors, the sound of shouting.

Sam waited for his breath to come back, staring at the place. Everything needed paint; boards on the front porch were missing.

He stopped then, his eyes going to the roof, pieces of slate cracked, but the two chimneys—

"My mother was teaching me numbers, I think," he said, the blur of her face in front of him. "I turned my head over the man's shoulder, the day we came, and I saw it on the house, *eleven*, and then a pair of chimneys, so huge up there in the sky. They looked like the number eleven too."

Just chimneys after all. Just the house number, the street number, of a terrible place that didn't exist anymore. And the woman who'd run the place was gone.

The doors were boarded. They walked around the back of the building and stopped to peer into the windows, to see rooms that were filled with broken furniture, dusty rooms that didn't mean anything. The kitchen was smaller than he remembered, the refrigerator gone, no boy with the flapping hands. Maybe he'd gone far away; he could be eleven now too. The poor boy who hadn't had a toy of his own.

"I don't belong here anymore. I think I never did," he said. "It's not my place."

He knew where he'd been, but what was most important was still missing. Mack.

20
Anima

"Take the notebook, Sam," Caroline said. They were standing on the corner near her house. There were tears in her eyes. "Learn to read, Sam. Then write to me."

He could feel the anger simmering. "Do you think I don't want to?" But this was Caroline, and he saw her face redden. "I'm sorry, really sorry," he said. "But I gave up on that."

"Draw pictures, put letters together any old way. Don't worry about the spelling. I'll understand it." The tears were running down her cheeks now, but she didn't pay attention to them.

"Maybe. I'll try." He knew he couldn't do it.

Would he ever see her again?

"One thing," he said, and she smiled, brushing the tears

away. "I would never have found out as much as I did without you."

He started down the street, and she called after him. "One thing. You'll be my best friend forever."

He raised one hand. He could hardly see her through his own tears. He turned the corner and began to run.

He stopped at the workroom door to say hello to Mack.

Mack looked up. "I'm sorry she's leaving," he said. "Such a nice girl. Anima's made something for you, crepes, I think."

Sam nodded, tried to smile. He walked along the back of the building, waving to Onji, and opened the kitchen door of Kerala House.

"Hey, sweetie." Anima looked up from the sink. "I've just made banana crepes for you, and we'll have a cup of tea." She pointed to a chair and put a plate in front of him.

How was he going to eat anything?

Anima gave a quick shake of her head, then poured tea for them both and sat opposite. She stirred a little sugar into her cup. "I'm sorry about Caroline," she said.

He took a gulp from his own cup. So much had happened today. "We took a bus to Waterway."

She glanced toward the window. "A long ride, but it was lovely out today. A day you'll remember."

He glanced at her. Waterway didn't mean anything to her, he could see that. For the first time he realized she might not know anything about where he came from. He took a breath. "Remember that sweater? Could I see it? Would you tell me about it?"

She blinked. "The little blue one with the zipper?" He knew she wanted to ask why, but instead she pointed up. "Eat the crepe. The sweater's upstairs."

Sam listened to her quick steps, the sound of a drawer opening. She brought the sweater back to the table and unwrapped the tissue paper around it.

They reached out at the same time to touch it. The wool was stiff, matted, the stitches pulled in spots.

"I want to know."

"About when you came?" Anima reached for his hand, held it with her own small one. "It was a terrible night, with sleet covering the roads, the sound of it against the windows." She shook her head. "Wait. Let me start at the beginning."

Her hand was even smaller than Caroline's. She bent her head and he could see a few strands of gray mixed in with the dark hair.

"I'd come here on my own from Kerala, and I had enough money from my parents to buy this building. But I was lonely, so lonely."

She made a chopping motion with one hand. "I had someone divide the building into three stores. Onji moved in first with Ellie; his wife had gone off somewhere. Later Ellie was married, and he was rattling around in the deli alone."

Anima patted Sam's hand. "One day, Onji came in. Right at this table, he told me his best friend, Mack, was on his way here, that he was moving from Florida. He needed a place to live and a place to work."

Anima tilted her head. "Onji said Mack was bringing a child from upstate somewhere."

She sighed. "Mack was supposed to come at dinnertime. We'd made all kinds of things, Onji and I, but he didn't come, and we waited, waited. We tried to eat the cold dinner, and we worried. I opened the door to see out, and everything was covered with a crust of ice. It was midnight, then two, three, and we sat here still. Just waiting."

His mouth was dry. *The boat? Had they been on the boat?*

"Just before light, Mack came in with you." Anima looked up. "And that cat. You were soaked, filthy; Mack looked exhausted. He'd hurt his leg somehow. When I tried to take you from him, he wouldn't let go. He sat down where you're sitting, Sam, rocking you, his head on your head. And his crying was a terrible thing to see."

Exhausted. That was the way Sam felt now. A long day.

"At last I took you." Her eyes were filled with tears. "I unzipped the sweater and pulled it off you. You were shivering now, and Mack, too. I found dry cloths, toweled you off. We put one of Onji's shirts on you. Huge. We've watched you grow into those shirts." She tapped his hand with one finger. "You became our family. We never felt lonely again." She sighed. "We never talked about that night again."

Sam stood up and went around the table. He leaned down to put his arms around her, smelling the sweet face cream she used, leaning his head against her thick hair. "I love you, Anima."

"I love you, too. We all do." She reached up and patted his cheek. "Would you like to take the sweater now?"

Sam shook his head. "You keep it for me."

He went outside and down to the water. Frogs floated on the surface, their throats swollen with song. Night Cat jumped up on Anima's bench, and Sam reached out to pet him. The cat had been lying in the sun, and his fur was warm.

Night Cat, who had come with him all the way.

Sam's Dream

Foghorns.
Freighters appearing, then disappearing in the mist.
Rocks.
A splintering noise.
The water level with the edge of the boat, black, cold.
Night Cat.
Water in his eyes, his mouth.
And then Mack.
"I've got you. You're safe."
Safe.
Safe.

21
Mack

Saturday again, early morning, and Caroline had been gone a week. Sam didn't bother with the kitchen light. He reached for the cereal box in the cabinet to stuff a handful into his mouth, then opened a can of tuna and dumped it onto Night Cat's plate.

In the workroom, he shoved up the windows. Outside, the air was still, and warm. Sam flexed his fingers. His hands were beginning to look like Mack's, to feel the way Mack's must feel. A callus had formed on his thumb from holding the plane. There was a small cut from a sharp edge of glass, paint under his nails; and a blue blister, perfectly round, had appeared on one finger.

He took the cover off the castle and picked up the

medieval woman, angling her inside Caroline's tangerine-colored room. He placed the pieces of roof over the towers and glued them carefully, one after another, circling the top of the castle; they fit well.

It was light now. A rim of sun appeared over the edge of the river. He rummaged through the small cans of paint, finding a charcoal color, and one a lighter shade. He experimented with them, painting on a piece of wood, then swiping at the wood with cloth so the color would look less flat, more like old stone.

Taking short, even strokes, he began to paint. The wood was smooth, and the pieces he had joined were tight and even.

It was soothing work, and he found himself humming the way Mack always did, stopping to touch the small trees he and Caroline had fashioned from bits of soap pads dipped in green paint, the gravel that made the path around the castle, and the small mirror that had become the moat.

He half-listened to the sounds around him, the call of two mourning doves outside, pots banging into each other at Onji's. And over Sam's head, Mack moved around, the bed creaked, a shoe dropped.

Sam stepped back. The first coat of paint was dry already. He went over to the sink to wash out the brush and had begun the second, lighter coat when he heard Mack at the workroom door, the intake of his breath. "Sam?"

Mack walked over to Sam's table. He reached out and touched the castle with one finger: the towers, the tiny windows, the smooth face. "Beautiful work," he said at last, his voice thick. "The work of a craftsman."

Sam looked up.

"It's Boldt Castle," Mack said.

"Yes." Sam thought of the day he and Caroline had named it. "How did you know?"

"How could I not know?" Mack said, almost as if he were talking to himself. He raised his hand to run it through his thick hair. "You've made it look like stone, and I can almost see water in the moat. But how did you remember? So long ago."

Remember. Sam stood still. Remember a castle?

Mack touched one of the tower roofs. "How did you know how to do this? To cut the pieces this way?"

"Anima's book," Sam said absently. "But, Mack—"

The back door opened, and Onji's footsteps came down the hall toward them.

Sam wanted to reach out and close the workroom door. He wanted to ask Onji to go away, to please not be there just now, because he was so close to finding out what he needed to know. And the rest of the story would take only a few minutes. He saw it in Mack's face, in Mack's blue eyes that were clouded with tears.

But Onji stood in the doorway. Onji, who talked, who always talked, didn't say a word. It was Mack who said, "The first time I put a hammer into his hand, I knew how it was going to be. The same for me—"

Onji came closer. "He remembered the castle."

"Yes," Mack said.

Sam took one step, and then a second, backing up against the wall with the shelves. He didn't make a sound; he was entirely still even inside himself, except for the pulsing in his throat and in his chest.

"It's so much like Boldt Castle. The windows, the towers . . ." Onji's voice trailed off.

Mack nodded with the barest movement of his head.

"So, Mack, I'm going back to my place," Onji said. "Maybe you'll want to talk now. Maybe you'll want to say things to Sam."

So Onji had known the whole story.

There was no sound in the workroom after Onji's footsteps died away, only that coo of the mourning doves outside, and the quick *la-la-lee* of a red-winged blackbird.

Night Cat must have felt the silence too. He jumped off the windowsill, onto Sam's table, and made himself a place next to the castle.

"I don't remember. Not all of it." Sam's voice sounded strange to himself. "Please—"

Mack's sigh was so loud it seemed to take up all the space in the room. He picked up one of the knights. "I should have told you before, but I thought you didn't remember, and I didn't want to tell you what a mess—" He began again. "What a terrible mess I made of everything."

Sam didn't move, even though the sharp corner of the shelf was digging into his shoulder.

"So much began because I was angry," Mack said.

"You're never—"

"A long time ago."

Mack touched the castle again. "I built a sailboat when I was young. I bought the wood, pieces at a time, I cut and sanded, fitted it all together. It took years."

"In the Thousand Islands," Sam said before he could stop himself.

Mack bent his head. "It was a perfect boat to sail through the waters of the St. Lawrence, to maneuver around those islands, around Heart Island. A narrow boat that responded so quickly in the mist—"

Sam closed his eyes. *Freighters' horns back and forth, one after the other, warning in the fog.* And hadn't that woman who'd come into the shop asked about Heart Island?

"Some of those islands were so large you couldn't see where they began or ended. And there was one that had only enough soil to fly a flag."

A little tuft of land. A flag whipping in the wind.

"We'll go back now. Today. Back to the Thousand Islands, back to the castle." He touched Sam's shoulder. "Back to where it all began."

22
Heart Island

They crossed a bridge into Gananoque on the Canadian side of the St. Lawrence. Mack parked the truck, and they sat on a bench near the water. The bag with Onji's lunch lay between them as they waited for a ferry to take them to the castle.

Sam glanced out at the pier, at the wisps of mist that rose above the river, and watched a small boat slapped by the waves as Mack began to talk. "We lived on the American side, and I kept the sailboat there," he said. "But we always came to this town, to Gan, Lydia and Onji and I." He talked slowly, looking out at the water. "There was a bulletin board every summer, telling who'd caught the largest muskie." He put his large hand on Sam's shoulder. "That's not important."

The muskie was more important than Mack knew, the word *muskie*. Hadn't it brought them here?

The picture of the sailboat was in Sam's pocket, and he pulled it out, seeing it tremble slightly in his fingers.

Mack ran his hand over it, almost the way Anima had run hers over the sweater. "My boat." He turned to face Sam. "How did you find it?"

Sam hesitated. "I climbed up into the attic."

"You went up the pipe?"

"I lied about it afterward—" He stopped and began again. "I'm sorry about that, about the lying."

"The pipe," Mack repeated. "And you found everything that was there? The little boat? I'd meant to give it back to you someday. But as time went on, it got harder. And you never asked."

"No one else could have built that boat."

Mack put his arm around Sam. "There's so much more to tell." He stopped and pointed. In the distance, a gleaming white ferry had appeared on the river, its horn sounding. A familiar sound.

Mack sighed. "When I was young I was always angry. Angry over foolish things. Angry until I brought you home to Anima and Onji. And then the anger seeped out of me like sap from a tree. But it was too late to mend things with my daughter; it's my worst regret."

The ferry had angled its way to the pier; the blast of the horn was all that could be heard.

Aboard the ferry, they climbed to the top deck. The mist

was stronger, sheets of it spread across the water as the ship pulled out slowly, almost lumbering.

Mack was talking about the castle now. "Boldt was the name of a man who changed the shape of the island into a heart for his wife, and you'll see the stone deer called harts."

They passed islands and then went under a bridge that curved upward like a steel cobweb. It must have been the bridge that Onji had described. And there, suddenly, was the castle Sam had dreamed about.

"Three hundred men worked there every day," Mack said. "But the day George Boldt's young wife died, everything stopped. He never went back."

They left the ferry and climbed a gravel path. "Years later, I was one of the workers who began to restore it," Mack said.

Sam glanced up at the towers, the roofs like cones, the narrow windows cut into the stone. If only Caroline could have seen it. Mack, smiling down at him, nodded. "Yes, it's like yours."

They wandered through the rooms. It was cold inside, but there was a fire in the massive fireplace. They sat on a bench watching the flames, and Mack took a breath. "You came here often. Your mother brought you. You'd follow me, the sound of your footsteps so loud, going up the stairs and down. You watched everything, squeezing in to see me hammer . . ."

If only he could remember.

"Everything was my fault," Mack said. "We argued over

149

something, my daughter and I, and I left and went to Florida. I lost my daughter, lost you, lost everything."

Wait. Sam felt his teeth going into his lip. Mack's words echoed in his head: *"Your mother brought you. . . . I lost my daughter, lost you."*

Sam's clenched hands went up to his face.

He knew. He didn't have to wait to be told. He tried to speak, but the sound wouldn't come. "My mother," he began at last, "was your daughter? Was really your daughter."

Mack turned, shock in his eyes. "Julia, of course. How could you not have known? I built the little boat for you in her kitchen."

Something was filling Sam's chest, growing, coming up into his throat. He opened his mouth, and a sound came.

Mack's arms were tight around him again, the heat from the fireplace warming him. "Oh, Sam," Mack said.

Sam was crying now, but whatever had filled his chest began to melt, to seep away with the tears. *"Like sap from a tree."* "It was your voice shouting."

"When?"

"At the Children's Home. Banging doors, one after the other."

"I was so angry," Mack said. "In a rage. That woman. How can I ever tell you? How can I explain? When your mother died, no one knew where I was, so a neighbor took you to the home. But then they found me." He ran his hand over his face. "Shocking, the packet that came in the mail: a loving note from Julia written just before she died, and legal papers giving me the right to take care of you, to raise you."

He was quiet for a moment. "I'd missed you, thought about you both all the time."

Sam wiped his face with his sleeve. It was all right, it was going to be all right.

"I came up on the boat to get you. I never stopped, never slept. You'd been in the home for almost a month, and that night, the woman wouldn't let me have you. 'I'm tired,' she said. 'Come back tomorrow.'

"I waved the court papers in front of her. I said you weren't going to stay there one more night, one more hour.

" 'Legal or not, you'll wait until tomorrow. He's in bed, and that's where I'm going soon. I'm not getting any child ready now. I've done my work for the day.' "

Sam pictured her face: she had lines across her forehead, and her hair was flat against her head.

"That terrible place." Mack raised his hand to his chest. "I can't tell you how angry I felt."

That something inside.

"I took the stairs two at a time. I opened one door after another—"

"You called, shouted."

"I wrapped you in a sweater and scooped you up in my arms, you and the boat, and went down the stairs. 'Night Cat,' you said."

Sam nodded, remembering the stairs tilting, his arm out, wanting the cat.

"The woman blocked the way into the kitchen, where Julia's cat was cowering under the table. Blocked the way until she saw my face."

They sat back, the flames crackling in the great room of the castle. Mack's eyes were closed. He seemed out of breath.

"I took you to the boat," Mack said.

"I remember the sound of foghorns," Sam said.

"I was too angry to think straight, or I wouldn't have taken you out in the storm. We went onto the rocks, the hull split, and the boat went under, all of it. We were in the water, and I reached out for you and the cat. Somehow you'd held on to the little boat I'd made." Mack's mouth was unsteady. "I nearly lost you the second time."

They went outside then, Sam feeling the wonder of it. They watched the moat below them, the boathouse across the way, swirls of mist.

"We took a train then to Onji and Anima," Mack said. "Both of us were soaked, the cat shivering. There was a nurse who sat nearby and bandaged my leg. I never thought what people would think. And then I carried you the last mile and they were waiting. And you were safe."

"Safe."

"I told myself I'd never go near the water again," Mack said. "I'd never have a boat again."

He smiled at Sam. "The next day we heard about the newspaper report." He shook his head. "Onji and I went back to let them know we were alive."

What Sam was feeling inside was a burst of happiness. He and Mack belonged together. Julia was his mother, Lydia his grandmother.

He realized what Mack had said. *"Never have a boat again."* He put his hand on Mack's sleeve. "Don't say that. Let's build a boat. The two of us, together."

23
The Festival

In the mornings, Sam still awoke before it was light. *Go back to sleep*, he told himself, yawning. The castle was finished, after all. He closed his eyes, but there was one more thing he might do for Caroline, even if she never knew it.

He nudged Night Cat lightly with his foot. The cat climbed over him and jumped off the bed to wait at the bedroom door.

Sam went downstairs into the kitchen and shredded a little leftover chicken for the cat, and took a roll for himself.

He still thought of Caroline. If only he could tell her the whole story.

In front of the castle, he plugged in the small cutters, listening to their buzz, and cut a rectangle into the front of the castle over the curved doors. Enough glass was left for one more window.

He smoothed the edges of the opening, fit the glass into it, and framed it by gluing on small pieces of wood. He stepped back.

The medieval lady was visible now; she stood in the tangerine room, looking out. *Making friends with the world instead of hiding,* he told Caroline in his mind.

He stood there, looking at the castle, satisfied. It could go upstairs now, maybe with the little boat on his dresser.

Mack was at the door. "Isn't today the school party?"

Pease porridge hot. Trenchers. Cloves and cinnamon.

"The medieval feast." Sam shrugged.

"I'll drive you in the truck, Sam. You won't be able to carry—"

"The castle? I'm not going to bring it."

"But why?"

Sam shook his head. He'd really made the castle for Caroline and for himself.

Mack glanced at the castle. "I always thought it was a shame that Boldt never finished his castle, that for years it just crumbled away."

"It isn't like that. I finished it, all of it."

Mack touched the small green book on the corner of the table. "Caroline wrote it down about building it. Didn't she? And shouldn't everyone know about that?"

Mack went to the door, tapping on the frame. "I'm going

to scramble some eggs, not as good as Onji's, but still—" He reached out. "Take the castle to school today, Sam. You'll be glad afterward."

How could Sam say no to Mack? He ripped out the back pages of the notebook, the section that belonged just to him, and took them up to his bedroom.

After breakfast they left for school a little late because it had taken so long to wrap the castle and put it in the back of the truck.

"Want me to come inside?" Mack asked as they unloaded it at the side door, but Sam shook his head. Without thinking, he reached out to hug Mack. He carried the castle down the hall alone, maneuvering his way around kids who were carrying cans of water for plants, kids who quickstepped instead of running, because Mr. Ramon might be lurking around the stairs.

In the classroom, Sam put the castle, still covered, on the table under the window. The room was noisier than usual. Five kids were getting ready to do their play, and Eric marched back and forth with his sword and a paper helmet that made Sam laugh. In the corner, Marcy practiced her oral report, her lips moving, her arms waving.

Stacked on the table were the large round pieces of bread with the centers scooped out, the trenchers Mrs. Stanek had promised she'd make. She'd actually brought in a huge pot of mashed peas to put on the bread, although Sam couldn't imagine anyone eating any of it. Marcy's mother had brought apple juice with cloves and Eric's mom had made a cinnamon cake, all food that had been around in the Middle Ages.

Mrs. Stanek turned and saw him. "You've finished the castle, Sam." She said it as if she'd known all along it would happen.

He stood there, embarrassed, not knowing what to do with his hands.

"Show us," she said.

He unwrapped the castle slowly, setting Caroline's horse straighter on the base, feeling the heat in his face.

Mrs. Stanek moved away from the board and came to the table, her hand to her mouth. "Oh, Sam." She touched the small knights standing in front, the towers, and bent over to see the medieval lady standing in the window. "It's Caroline, isn't it?"

"Her mother made them, and Caroline made the horse," he said. "It's all here in her notebook."

"Hey, look at what Sam did," Marcy said, and then everyone was crowding in to look at the castle, looking at him. "Cool," someone said, and "Sam built this?" someone else said.

Eric grinned at him. "Terrific, MacKenzie. Really terrific."

Sam couldn't stop grinning back at Eric, and at the rest of them. Mack had been right. Sam went back to his seat, glad that he'd brought the castle. More than glad.

Marcy began her speech, talking about cities with walls built around them for protection. And Mrs. Stanek walked around the room passing out her trenchers, holding out the pot of peas.

Sam took a trencher. "I'll try the peas." He'd probably be the only one, but after all, Anima made something delicious with chickpeas—how different could this be? Besides, Mrs. Stanek's face was red. For the first time he thought about how hard she tried.

The peas were terrible, with enough pepper to make him sneeze, but he didn't have time to think about it, because the classroom door banged open, and Marcy stopped speaking, one arm raised.

Caroline stood there, her bracelets circling halfway up her arm. She was wearing a purple hat that curled around her face. As if no one else were in the room, she smiled at him, and said, "Here I am, Sam-I-Am."

24
Mrs. Waring

The dismissal bell rang. Sam zigzagged down the hall, carrying one end of the castle. "Those trenchers. Ugh."

Caroline zigzagged behind him with the other. "I'll tell Mom it was worth that two-hour drive this morning just to taste those peas. Yum." They laughed.

Sam backed down the three outside steps, trying to hold the castle level.

"Easy," Caroline said, and then, "So what about Sam Bell?"

"It was my parents' name." He bent to pick up a knight that had slid off the edge of the castle. "But Mack thought it would be easier for me to have his."

They reached the van, and Caroline's mother popped the rear door from the driver's seat.

"You're sure it's all right?" Caroline asked.

Sam grinned at her. "About my name? About the castle? Sure."

"One thing. I know why you put the window in my room in the castle."

He waited.

"You want me to look for friends. Don't you?"

"Just go to the classroom door. Just pick out a kid, and smile. You have a great smile. You'll see." He slid the castle into the rear of the van.

"Oh, Sam," she said. "I will. I'll never forget—" She did smile then. "Thanks. But one more thing. How can we stay friends if you don't e-mail, if you don't write?"

She put a crumpled piece of paper in his hand. "My e-mail address." She leaned forward—purple hat, a dozen bracelets, a constellation of freckles—and kissed his cheek before she went around to the front of the van. "Think about it. Write to me. I'll figure it out. Say yes."

He stepped back to stand on the curb, his hand raised to his face, watching until they pulled away and turned the corner. He went back into school and down the stairs to the Resource Room.

Mrs. Waring was at the window, watering her plants.

"I have to read," he said.

"Sam?" She brushed a drop of water off a leaf. "I saw your castle at lunchtime. Everyone's talking about it, and no wonder. It's amazing."

"Thanks, but listen, I don't have to be a great reader, but I have to get by."

Her head was tilted, the watering can dripping.

How could he tell her the whole story? The papers in the attic, the computer, Caroline, all of it? What a difference it would have made if he could have read? He settled for telling her just about the boat. "My grandfather and I are going to build a sailboat. I want to write it down. What we do, how we do it."

"How much time did you spend thinking about that castle? How much time working on it?"

He knew what she was thinking. "Every minute I had."

"That's what it takes sometimes." She put the watering can down and wiped her fingers on her jeans, then lifted the pot off the C and traced it with her finger. "How about giving me a couple of afternoons every week after school, a couple of mornings for part of the summer? We'll keep at it, work on it; we'll really try." She held out her hand. "Give me a chance, Sam. I love to teach the way you love to build."

She had such a nice smile, her teeth a little crooked, her dark eyes soft. All right, he could do that.

He swept his hand around the room. "And sometime soon, I'll make shelves for this room."

He'd missed the bus again, but that was all right too. It was warm out, almost summer, so he jogged part of the way.

Mack was outside, waiting for him. They walked out back to stand in the doorway of the shed. Piles of sweet-smelling wooden planks stretched from one end to the other, and boxes of screws and nails were stacked against the wall. Mack had begun the cradle that would hold the growing hull of the boat.

They breathed in the sweetness of the wood, half-listening to the music that was coming from Anima's restaurant. Sam flexed his fingers; he couldn't wait to begin. But Onji poked his head out the window. "Plenty of time for that. First, how about some muffins, you guys, and a glass of milk? Put some meat on those bones."

"We're built that way in our family," Mack said. "Thin but tough."

"Right," Sam said.

They opened the back door of the deli. "Just a second," Sam said. He went into Onji's office to get to the Internet and smoothed out the paper with Caroline's address. He wanted to be sure she'd get the first message as soon as she reached home. One thing. One word. Yes.

So eleven.

It could be anything.
A street, a house number, a pair of chimneys that didn't
frighten him anymore.
His eleventh birthday.
The year he met his best friend.
It might even be the double masts on the boat
he'd sail every summer on the St. Lawrence,
with all of them, Mack, Onji, Anima, and Caroline.
It was the year he began to read.

Acknowledgments

To Wendy Lamb, my editor, who guided me through the book with wonderful patience,

To George Nicholson, my agent, who cheered me on,

To Dave Southard, who told me about the mist, and the foghorns, and the freighters on the St. Lawrence, and made it all come alive in my mind,

To Kathy Winsor Bohlman, my friend, for her interest and help,

To my children:

Jim, who "book talks" with me,

Bill, who read and reread, and gave me wonderful suggestions,

Alice, who read gently,

To my grandchildren, all seven, who keep me rooted in their world,

and to Jim, my husband, who believes in me.

Love and thanks to all of you.

About the Author

Patricia Reilly Giff is the author of many beloved books for children, including the Kids of the Polk Street School books, the Friends and Amigos books, and the Polka Dot Private Eye books. Several of her novels for older readers have been chosen as ALA Notable Books and ALA Best Books for Young Adults. They include *The Gift of the Pirate Queen; All the Way Home; Nory Ryan's Song*, a Society of Children's Book Writers and Illustrators Golden Kite Honor Book for Fiction; *Maggie's Door;* and the Newbery Honor Books *Lily's Crossing* and *Pictures of Hollis Woods*. *Lily's Crossing* was also chosen as a *Boston Globe–Horn Book* Honor Book. Her most recent books are *A House of Tailors; Willow Run*, the companion to *Lily's Crossing;* and *Water Street*, the companion to *Nory Ryan's Song* and *Maggie's Door*.

Patricia Reilly Giff lives in Connecticut.